THE MINAS DECEPTION

A Scott Stiletto Thriller 5

BRIAN DRAKE

WOLFPACK
PUBLISHING
— EST 2013 —

WOLFPACK
PUBLISHING
— EST 2013 —

Published in the United States by Wolfpack Publishing, Las Vegas

Wolfpack Publishing
6032 Wheat Penny Avenue
Las Vegas, NV 89122

wolfpackpublishing.com

Paperback ISBN 978-1-64119-832-5
eBook ISBN 978-1-64119-831-8

Library of Congress Number: 2019946332

THE MINAS DECEPTION

For the people of Venezuela fighting for their freedom against extreme odds.

CHAPTER ONE

Somewhere in Venezuela

The deuce-and-a-half chugged along the two-lane road at a moderate speed, black smoke belching from the raised exhaust pipes on either side of the cabin. The camouflage paint blended the machine with the forest.

The canopy over the back had been removed, and four Americans decked out in combat fatigues with automatic rifles sat with six similarly dressed and armed Hispanic men. All eyes scanned the road and the forest along either side of it.

CIA officer Tim Pierce shifted on the narrow and uncomfortable bench. He glanced at the rebel soldiers. Their faces showed various levels of exhaustion after their afternoon training effort, but they were still watching for threats. Twenty miles remained before they reached home base, and Pierce couldn't wait to get back to the relatively safe confines of the camp. If nothing else, they'd have more men handy if the enemy showed up for a hammer party.

Pierce's team and his three CIA contractors (he was the only full-time Agency employee) had been sent to Venezuela to train the rebel forces who were locked in a fight with the country's dictator, one Lazaro Minas. Minas ruled with an iron fist while portraying himself to the rest of the world, on whom he depended for foreign aid and other means of support, as a duly-elected leader of a prosperous population. What the rest of the world didn't see were the death squads who targeted all manner of dissenters, the poverty spreading like a virus across the nation, and the sleight-of-hand tricks Minas employed to hide the truth from those he fooled. Dissenters not murdered by the death squads often found themselves in work camps, while those in poverty were left to suffer. Minas and his cronies enriched themselves with most of the foreign aid, yet continued to provide lip service, and now and then some crumbs, to the dependent population.

Pierce didn't dislike the assignment, but the hot weather was merciless. His skin was slick with sweat under his fatigues, made worse by his heavy uniform and combat harness, neither of which had been designed with the comfort of the wearer in mind, much like the bench on which he sat hadn't been designed for the comfort of the sitter. The rest of the crew wasn't faring much better, with some of the rebels sweating through their battle dress tops, buttons left undone to let in some air. Military discipline mandated they not do so, but Pierce understood their reasoning and didn't say anything to the contrary.

The rebels were eager to learn and itching for a fight, and they wanted Minas out of power and replaced. They wanted their freedom. There was nothing about that attitude with which Pierce could argue. He was an Annapolis grad who had grown up on the water, mostly fishing with his grandfather, so the Navy had seemed like a natural choice when he decided to make a career of serving his country. He could have enjoyed a long career as an officer, commanding a ship or riding a desk at the Pentagon, but Pierce had strong ideals about freedom and man's right to have it. Freedom wasn't a gift from a government, but a right decreed by God. More often than not, the SEALs were the ones to liberate the oppressed before anybody else arrived (sorry, Marines) and that was where Pierce wanted to focus his effort. After his career with the SEALs came to an end, he was left to contemplate a civilian job, or apply at one of the many private contracting companies doing Uncle Sam's business in various world hotspots. Instead, he answered a call from McLean, Virginia, and the office of CIA's Special Activities Division. Now, after ten years in the Navy and another ten as a spy, he found himself still doing what he did best. In Venezuela.

His role was, for now, limited to training and advising. Pierce hoped the US took a more active role later, and that he and his crew were paving the way for an eventual large-scale deployment. Venezuela was ripe for a regime change. He'd seen the horror of the Minas terror machine first-hand. The rebel leaders had taken the Americans on a "tour," so to speak, and Pierce had reported back to Washington that the rumored death squads were quite real, the population was very much under the boot of a murderer, and they seriously needed to do something about the situation.

The reply? Follow your orders.

Fair enough, Pierce decided. But maybe later. . .

The deuce jolted along the road, everybody in the back bouncing, grabbing for any hold available to keep from falling off the bench seat. The road wasn't entirely smooth, and the worn shocks and springs had long since stopped shielding riders from the bumps.

Pierce, his team, and the rebels had been running fast-attack and ambush drills throughout most of the day, stopping only for a short lunch, and now they were heading back to one of the main base camps to rest up for the next round of drills, which would include a different group of rebels for nighttime maneuvers. The leaders of the resistance forces didn't want too many of their troops away from camp at one time in case of an attack, which happened frequently. The rebels were always on the move.

And then a fiery blast erupted from the center of the roadway. The blast destroyed the cabin, enveloping the driver and passenger in a ball of flame as the steel structure dissolved into pieces of deadly shrapnel. The front of the vehicle lifted skyward, the deuce almost tipping over, and Pierce, his contract team, and the rebels were flung from the back and onto the road. They landed hard, bones snapping, heads cracking, men screaming, some continuing to roll across the pavement, and a few landing with such finality that they did not move at all.

Gravity took hold and pulled the front of the deuce back to the pavement with a crash. Flames engulfed the undercarriage, tearing at the rubber and steel, and the roadway filled with choking black smoke that slowly drifted skyward. The light wind pushed the smoke into the forest.

Pierce heard moaning. He hurt everywhere and he tried to move, but the pain was too much. His legs didn't seem broken; he could move them, but not very much.

His rifle was nowhere near him. He reached for the SIG-Sauer P-226 on his right hip as uniformed soldiers emerged from the jungle. He counted seven. He'd loaded his pistol with a 20-round extended magazine of +P extra-pressure 9mm hollow-points. He could take them. The enemy held their rifles at the ready, stalking to the fallen bodies with purpose. Pierce raised his pistol. Two of his teammates made moves for their own pistols.

"Put down the weapons," the leader of the soldiers said, a man who didn't hold a rifle, but instead wore a holstered sidearm and had general's stars on his shoulders. He stopped at the edge of the pavement. Mud spotted his wrinkled uniform; his boots, in particular, were covered in dried brown muck. It told Pierce that they had been waiting in ambush for quite some time.

How had they known?

"This is not a fight you can win. You are brave men for trying, and I would expect nothing less from professional soldiers, but I also expect you to recognize when the odds are against you."

Pierce lined the three-dot sight on the man's chin. The man looked at him without smiling, without blinking, his eyes daring him to fire. He either wasn't afraid of being shot, or he knew Pierce didn't have the strength to pull the trigger. Pierce clenched his teeth and felt the muscles in his index finger force back the SIG's trigger. The bearded man waited.

And then Pierce's arm started to shake. The pain from his impact with the ground finally overtook him. He didn't want to drop the gun, but it fell from his grip anyway as he pulled his arm to his body and stifled a groan. The pavement felt hot against his left cheek.

This is a lousy place to die.

"That's better," the general said. "You are now prisoners of Presidente Lazaro Minas, our great leader, who wishes only to be left alone and not harassed by Americans. You will be treated most harshly for your interference in our country, and you will probably not survive."

The general tossed back his head and laughed heartily. His laugh echoed mockingly, but he didn't look so tough any longer. Pierce flexed the fingers of his right hand. If only...

The other enemy soldiers moved in like hungry sharks, fingers on the triggers of their Kalashnikov AK-12 automatic rifles. Pierce knew the weapon as the latest and greatest from Russia, a tidbit Washington would want to know. The troopers' eyes communicated quite clearly that they were going to follow orders, but also wouldn't mind shooting anybody who tried to fight. Pierce was powerless to stop them as they began dragging him, his men, and the rebels out of the roadway.

The fire continued eating at the destroyed truck, the metal groaning under the intense heat of the flames. A plume of smoke filled the sky long after they were gone.

The sprawling hacienda that served as the home of El Presidente Lazaro Minas was shaped like a V. It was two stories tall, and Minas designed it himself. It sat on a hillside overlooking the capital of Caracas, visible to the population below at all times. El Presidente's specifications had called for palm trees and they dotted the property, their splendor a testament to Venezuela's good soil. The ground behind the tip of the V sloped down and contained a large garden of colorful plant life, marble statues, a maze of hedgerows, a large swimming pool, and a patio area.

More soldiers than palm trees surrounded the property right now, and from his perch on the second floor deck overlooking the manicured lawn and the long driveway connecting to the main road, General Vitorio Florez, having returned from capturing the American spies, wondered for the umpteenth time what he would do with the hacienda had it been his property. Minas preferred understated decoration; Florez' tastes were louder, more obnoxious, and gaudy.

Give it time. . .

Venezuela had recently suffered the wrath of Hurricane Margaret, and there wasn't one spot of the country untouched by her destruction. The hurricane had raged for three days, only one of those on land, but the residual tropical storm had left a great deal of the country flooded. Most of the debris around the hacienda had already been cleared away, and the green grass was back to its former splendor. Trim pieces on the house that the wind had carried away had been quickly and dutifully replaced, and soon the whole exterior would be repainted, but for now, yard crews tended to the palm trees that had snapped under the hurricane's onslaught. The damaged trees were being uprooted and replaced, the crews working steadily, as if they'd get their heads lopped off if they didn't finish the job on time. Florez smiled. Maybe they would. One never knew what El Presidente might do to somebody who displeased him. But because one could never be sure a supposedly loyal tree surgeon wasn't also a rebel, General Florez had ordered more soldiers to the property than usual. Just in case. Rebel activity had calmed down in recent weeks, mostly due to American interference with a CIA team in-country to allegedly "train" rebel soldiers, but the last thing Florez wanted to do was cause Minas to get angry by opening the hacienda to attack.

The rebels could blow up anything else they wanted, but if they touched the hacienda. . .

Florez didn't want to think about the consequences.

He needed to keep order while Minas was in New York City, talking to the United Nations. It was a burdensome task, one that demanded more hours than the day made available. Florez now understood while Minas required so many luxuries. Without such things to look forward to, one could not possibly lead.

He might get his own head lopped off if he failed to keep order. Or, worse, be sent to a work camp, where he'd be at the mercy of other prisoners if they weren't already starved beyond the ability to fight. But the sight of him, the man who put many of them in the work camps, might bring them back to life long enough to kill him.

That would be bad. He shook his head to clear the silliness from his thoughts. He didn't need to think about consequences because he knew how to do his job, do it well, and keep El Presidente happy. There was no need to speculate on what-ifs that were never going to happen.

Minas' mission in New York City had to succeed. The request for humanitarian aid to help the country recover from the hurricane was a con job, Florez knew. Some of the money might be spent on infrastructure repair, some would line the pockets of the leadership, and the rest would be invested in a new scheme of El Presidente's to attract a number of foreign investors to help Venezuela mine gold and other precious resources the country currently had no ability to dig up. The Russians had helped for a while, and it had seemed as if they would "adopt" Venezuela, but Minas' inability to pay them for their help ultimately upset the Kremlin enough that they ordered their people and equipment out. Now, more investment was required.

To Florez, the mining effort meant that dissent had to be dealt with more harshly than ever. They couldn't take the chance of rebels sabotaging the mining effort, which would bring untold millions into Venezuela's coffers. Right now was the perfect time to kill as many rebels as possible, perhaps even break the back of the resistance and send anyone who survived the death squads into hiding forever.

Florez gazed at the courtyard centered within the V. Minas had spared no expense in his design. The patio was paved with marble. Deathly slippery when it rained, but beautiful to look at when the sun shone. The water fountain in the center remained off. It had been damaged in the hurricane and needed repair. That was next on the list. El Presidente wasn't expecting it to be done before he returned home, however. The priority job was replacing his beloved palm trees.

Florez pondered the courtyard some more. It was hard not to dream of his own luxuries when overlooking El Presidente's extravagance. Maybe someday he could replace the marble with something as nice but less ridiculous.

He'd keep the fountain, though. The trickling water helped provoke peaceful contemplation. Sometimes a warrior needed that. A leader certainly did.

Somewhere in Rome

Scott Stiletto parked his rental on a side street and left the car unlocked. He didn't intend to be gone long enough to give a potential car thief a chance to take the vehicle.

His mental countdown began as he rounded a corner and started up the sloping sidewalk to the front entrance of an apartment building, one of many such dwellings sandwiched together on the narrow street. The outside of the target building had been painted white, and it had wood trim around the windows facing the street. All of the windows were closed against the warm air and thick humidity.

A compact car approached from the opposite direction, the driver carefully navigating to pass the line of cars parked on the left-hand side of the road. Parked as they were, the cars took up a large portion of the cobblestone street. One could not drive at speed through this neighborhood, or not safely, anyway. Stiletto needed to get in and out of the neighborhood without endangering civilians.

The enemy, of course, had no such restrictions.

Stiletto moved fast and almost regretted the effort. He wore a leather jacket to conceal his pistol, but the sunny

Roman day, accompanied by the eighty-percent humidity, was making him sweat hard. He opened the door of the apartment building, glad for the blast of air conditioning, and ignored the elevator. Instead, he turned right and pushed through a door to the stairwell. As he ascended to the third floor, he palmed a ViperTek VTS-979 stun gun he'd put up his right sleeve. Wrapping his fingers around the contoured grip, he placed his thumb on the go-button that set off the electric charge.

A quiet hallway greeted him as he stepped out of the stairwell, and he counted doors until he found apartment 306. He used his left hand to knock, holding the stun gun behind his right leg.

The chain rattled, the deadbolt snapped, and the door opened about two inches. A young man's face appeared in the gap. He had a narrow face with a mop of black hair and a dark mole under his nose. Stiletto kicked the door and it slammed into the man, who fell back with a startled grunt. Stiletto stepped through the doorway and kicked the door shut in one smooth motion. The other man started to rise, and Scott jammed the ViperTek into the man's belly and pressed the trigger button. The taser snapped the life, the crackling jolt of electricity filling the room. The young man's eyes widened for a moment, then clamped shut as his body rapidly convulsed and contracted on itself, the man folding into a fetal position. Then he was still, minus the occasional spasm. Stiletto pulled back. The man, his mouth slack, was already drooling into the carpet.

Stiletto dropped the ViperTek into the inside pocket of his jacket and surveyed the room.

He spotted what he'd come for right away.

A leather briefcase rested on a coffee table in the living room off the kitchen, the lid open. Stiletto went over to the table. A stainless-steel canister rested in foam padding within the case. Scott didn't need to see anything more. He'd been on the trail of the young man and his goon squad for over a month. Today was the climax of his recent efforts.

The chatter stream had lately been full of talk of a canister of uranium for sale, specifically a sample of Uranium-235 from an unknown source. The amount for sale was enough to entice any jihadist or other terrorists who wanted to build a dirty bomb. Scott had tracked down the group of Italians selling the U235, a group connected with the old Red Brigade. They were a splinter cell that was trying to reignite a terrorist campaign in Europe in general, and Italy in particular. But they needed money, and the U235 sale was said to be part of a funding program for their larger operations.

Stiletto had been too young to battle the original Red Brigade back in the '70s and '80s, but he knew their reputation well. The communist group had been responsible for a slew of murders on Italian soil, namely government officials, but a few civilians had died by their guns too. They'd been stamped out in the late '80s, but rumors of Brigade members reforming and continuing their efforts to bring about a communist Italy continued.

Stiletto had followed the chatter to Rome and identified the players over a month's time, then conducted
surveillance on the group. He learned their habits and rou-
tines and noted their locations. When they finalized the
sale with the buyer, Stiletto went into action. The buyers
were Chechen terrorists who reportedly wanted to set off
a dirty bomb in Moscow.

Stiletto had no love for the Russians, particularly the
current regime. The Kremlin had placed a contract on his
life for illegally infiltrating the country and rescuing a
friend involved in planning a coup against the sitting president. The mission had been successful—Vlad Glinkov
and his family were safe in the United States, having
brought back valuable intelligence on Kremlin connec-
tions to Russian mafia groups in the US. But the mission
had come with a cost; the CIA, with whom he'd spent
many loyal years, had fired Stiletto. Now Scott roamed
the globe, his gun for sale, but never his soul. Some things
were worth more than money.

But the Kremlin wanted revenge, and badly. Stiletto
had forgotten the total amount of the contract, but he'd
managed to avoid major attempts on his life because he
never stopped looking over his shoulder.

He was free of CIA restraints and on his own, yes, but
he had no sense of peace any longer. He was a man always
at war, one way or another, and he had no idea how to sort
it out, short of turning himself over to Moscow, which he

had no plans to do.

All the same, he didn't want to see a dirty bomb set off in Moscow or anywhere else. He wouldn't allow innocent people to suffer, no matter who in their government had marked him for death for whatever reasons. He'd deal with the threat directly soon enough. Meanwhile, he had more important matters that required his attention.

He removed the canister and placed it on a shelf next to the wall-mounted flat screen television. Grabbing some heavy books from another nearby shelf, he ripped out the foam insert, and then placed the books in the case. Closing the lid, he tested the weight. It felt heavy, and would hopefully fool the Chechens long enough for him to close in for the kill.

The countdown clock in his mind continued ticking down. The young man's cell phone lay on the table next to the case. Stiletto picked up the phone, hoping there was no unlock code required, but there was. A thumbprint instead of a number code—very clever. He went over to the man and put his thumb against the screen, and the phone unlocked. Stiletto searched through his notes and confirmed the meet location—a McDonalds not far away—and the recognition code. He was also to have the briefcase on the left side of his table, and only order a coffee and two chocolate chip cookies.

Stiletto hated coffee.

Impossible mission, indeed.

Stiletto hurried out of the apartment, locking the door

behind him. With the case in his left hand, he went back down the stairwell to the street and returned to his rental car, placing the briefcase on the seat beside him.

As he drove out onto the narrow street once more, the windows rolled up and the A/C blasting, Stiletto used his cell phone to make a call. He wasn't using his personal cell, but instead, a pre-paid burner phone purchased at a grocery store. There was only one number programmed into it. He left a short message with the woman who answered, explaining that a member of the Red Brigade was unconscious in an apartment and that the U235 everybody was looking for was waiting on a shelf. The lady started to ask a question, and Stiletto cut off the call. Let the agents of AISI, Italy's internal security agency, pick up the ball. He'd wanted to leave the Red Brigader alive for further questioning, and the Italians would have that pleasure, along with claiming victory for intercepting the nuclear material.

Now it was time to handle the Chechens.

Stiletto turned left at the end of the street and picked up speed as he blended with traffic.

There were no free spaces in the restaurant parking lot. After two passes to make sure, Stiletto parked two blocks away.

He didn't like the idea of hoofing it on foot with a heavy briefcase. The humidity didn't help. You could cut the wet air with a knife. Stiletto's shirt stuck to his skin under the jacket. Stiletto had no control over the weather, so it was best to ignore the discomfort.

He only passed a few pedestrians on his way. The Italian language was something he hadn't heard in a long time, although he'd mostly heard Italian being shouted by his grandmother every time Grandpa had tried to put a finger in the fresh marinara sauce to have a taste. His father's side hailed from Italy, but he wasn't sure which region. His home growing up had been full of Italian tradition, but that wasn't something Stiletto continued to practice as an adult. A man living on his own only needed the basics. Had his family remained intact, had his original "plan" been successful—retire from the army and settle down with his wife and adult daughter—he'd certainly have revived some of his father's favorites. But life had other plans. Stiletto's wife, Maddy, had died, and his daughter had cut him out of her life, despite Stiletto's good-faith attempts to regain contact. Hopefully, someday she'd pick up the phone when he called. Joining the CIA had helped him adjust to the tragedy, and allowed him to do what he did best: serve his country. Now, on his own, he'd had to make further adjustments, and find new meaning for the words "serve" and "normal."

Some days he felt like he was making headway and finding a sense of normalcy.

Other days, none at all.

Maybe his family had come from Rome. Why not?

Maybe he didn't realize he was currently tracing the foot-steps of his great-great-grandfather by walking along the sidewalk. Heaven knew what his great-great-grandfather would have thought of McDonald's, an eyesore in the United States and hardly a welcome sight in Rome. But business was business, and apparently even Italians even-tually tired of pasta. The dining room was packed, but the chilly temperature inside was an obvious reason for the crowd. Stiletto wasn't the only one sick of sweating. A table opened while Stiletto waited in line, and he brought his steaming coffee and two chocolate chip cookies to the table by the window, which offered a view of the exit point of the drive-thru lane. Stiletto sat with his back to the glass, which was a glaring tactical error. His back-side was too big a target at that spot, and every instinct screamed for him to move at the first possible opportu-nity. However, the Chechens needed to see him. They needed to see the briefcase on his left, and he needed to see them. Getting shot in the back during the process of the exchange was something he'd have to risk, and deal with if it actually happened.

Stiletto was ready for a fight should the meeting take a disastrous turn. Not only did he still have the ViperTek stun gun, but his pistol rode in the shoulder harness under his left arm.

The Colt Combat Government .45 auto had seen a lot of hard use recently, so Stiletto'd had the gun refreshed by a gunsmith with new springs, small parts, and a new finish to cover the scratches. He'd also added an extended safety catch and new Tritium night sights.

He spotted the Chechens right away. Two men, trim, wearing windbreakers, both with dark hair and sharp eyes that scanned the room as they entered. Their faces were not smooth. They looked like men who had seen a lot and lived harshly. They looked like fighters. Stiletto knew only the basics of the conflict between the Russians and the Chechens. He understood that Russia felt the territory was theirs, and the Chechens disagreed. They wanted their own government, their own land, and the right to make their own decisions, albeit ones based on their current form of leadership, Stiletto thought, which violated basic human rights and made them as bad as any half-dozen villains he'd already encountered in his career.

Russia and Chechnya had fought two wars over the dispute, and Russian anti-terrorist units had wreaked havoc across the country trying to kill men like the ones Stiletto saw now. The Chechens had struck back with equal force within Moscow, and the death toll had risen on both sides. It was an old story, one repeated many times throughout history, and Stiletto often wondered when such fighting would stop. But he knew it never would. War was as basic to human nature as breathing. There was always somebody who wanted to control somebody else, and the opposite side who wanted no such restrictions on their lives. Those fighting the oppression, even if they didn't have guns, found some way, when possible, to fight back. Always.

Stiletto tried not to grimace as he slowly sipped his coffee and kept his eyes on the taller of the two. He'd rather drink Drano than coffee—the beverage simply wasn't palatable—but he had to play the part. Stiletto wanted to meet the man's eyes, get his attention, and have him see the briefcase. The crowd in the restaurant meant they'd have to walk around a bit. Making eye contact might quicken the process.

It did. The dark-haired man spotted Scott and his coffee cup. Stiletto swallowed the toxic liquid and set down the paper cup. He'd have to gargle with bleach later to get the taste out of his mouth, or at least Scope. Why couldn't the instructions have specified bathing in swamp water before the meeting?

The two Chechens did not order. They approached Scott's table, and the tall one sat down. The other stayed back a pace. Stiletto didn't like the look the man gave him.

"Why aren't you eating your cookies?" the Chechen said.

Stiletto sighed inwardly. It was the first half of the recognition code. Part of him had hoped such silliness had gone out with the Cold War, but apparently not.

He said, "It's better to share than keep it all to oneself."

The Chechen nodded. "You have it?"

"In the case."

The shorter man spoke sharply in Chechen. Stiletto wasn't sure which dialect he was using, as there were so many within the native language, but he couldn't mistake the look on the man's face. Had he missed something that now blew his cover? His pulse quickened. He kept his hands on the table despite the urge to grab the Colt .45.

The seated man said, "My partner says you aren't the man we're supposed to see."

"Right. He couldn't make it. Got his head caught in a trash compactor."

The Chechens didn't laugh.

"I'm kidding," Stiletto said. "Something else came up, and he asked me to take his place."

The shorter man spoke sharply again.

The tall man rose, lifting his jacket to show Stiletto the butt of a SIG-Sauer handgun.

"Come with us."

"That wasn't the deal."

"You'll be lucky if you survive this deal, my friend. Follow us."

"Can I bring my cookies?"

The tall man leaned forward, grabbed one of the cookies, and took a bite. As he straightened, his partner tugged on Stiletto's arm.

"I'll leave them, then," Scott said, rising.

The Chechens kept him between them as they exited the restaurant.

The Chechens grabbed Stiletto hard and shoved him into an alley a block from the restaurant. The shorter man was strong. He held Stiletto against a brick wall, his arms like steel, as the tall man took the case, popped the locks, and let the lid fall open. The books Stiletto had stashed inside tumbled to the ground.

The short man punched Stiletto in the gut, slamming his fist under the rib cage at an upward angle. Stiletto felt a flash of pain through his body as breath left him and he doubled over, choking. The short man reached under his jacket, ignoring the Colt, but finding the ViperTek stun gun. Scott grabbed for his auto pistol while still trying to suck air, but as his hand clamped around the butt of the .45, the stun gun crackled. Stiletto screamed as the twin bolts made contact with his skin through the fabric of his jeans. His legs fell out from under him, and he hit the ground with a thud.

Now Stiletto was drooling.

Maybe he shouldn't have laughed at the Red Brigader he'd tasered, who had immediately started drooling on his carpet. What goes around, comes around, and all that. Next time, he'd censor the snide remarks.

Or not. Who was he kidding?

His hands were taped behind his back. Duct tape. Not a solid way to restrain somebody, but it would do if there was nothing else, or until the tape could be replaced. Problem was, Stiletto knew how to break free. Pull hard enough, and duct tape breaks.

He lay on his side in the back of a van with blacked-out

windows. The Chechens were up front, the tall man driving, the shorter one in the passenger seat. When the short man looked back at Scott, he smiled and said something to his partner.

Stiletto swallowed. His whole body hurt, but it especially hurt where the prongs had stabbed into his leg, more than where the fist had landed in his belly.

The holster under his left arm was empty. He still had the spare magazines under his right arm, though.

"Which one of you has my gun?" Stiletto said.

The short Chechen looked at Scott, but neither replied.

"I'll want that back," Stiletto said. "Undamaged."

The two men did not reply.

The van jolted as it traveled along the streets, and Stiletto decided the Italians needed to spend less time sucking down vino and more time improving their roads. He wondered if the road they were traveling on had been around during Nero's reign. It sure felt like it had.

When the taller of the two Chechens turned the wheel to the left, the van jolted once again as it entered the back lot of a building. Stiletto saw some of it through the front windows, but nothing identified the structure. The outside had white paint. That he knew for sure. It was old paint, judging by some fading near the edge of the roof. The van stopped, and the two Chechens climbed out and opened the back doors. The tall one grabbed Stiletto by the ankles and dragged him along the floor to the chrome bumper, which was hot to the touch and burned through Stiletto's clothes. The short one held the Colt Combat Government. Stiletto said, "Are you sure you know how to handle that thing?"

The man grunted.

The tall one grabbed the now-closed briefcase with one hand, and the back of Stiletto's coat with the other and hauled him to his feet. He shoved Stiletto forward roughly, steering him by the shoulders to the back door of the building.

Now Stiletto identified the place—a nightclub, currently closed. Stiletto's shoes scraped on the asphalt as they neared the rear entrance, Shorty stepping ahead to twist a rusty knob and pull the door open. Scott noted contact wires on the doorframe. The rusty knob and bad paint on the door made the place look neglected, but they had high-tech security. Stiletto figured the security setup was cheaper than a new paint job.

Unless the club was a front for Chechen rebel activity and the outward appearance didn't matter.

The doorway led straight to the dance floor. Tables sat atop chairs, and the bright lights gave the nightclub a large, open feeling. The few times Stiletto had visited such places during operating hours with their dim lights, they'd always seemed cramped.

"Who is this?" asked a thick Caucasian man in dark clothes. The man stood behind a mixing console near the dance floor. He put down some tools.

Shorty said, "I made our deal with Francois. This man

showed up instead."

The tall Chechen shoved Stiletto hard. Scott couldn't stop himself from falling painfully onto the cold dance floor. He did use the opportunity to further stretch the tape holding his wrists together and rolled onto his side, gasping.

The boss stepped closer.

"Why is this a big deal?" he said. "Francois couldn't make it, so what?"

"He doesn't know that I know Francois," Shorty said. "He would have called to tell us."

"And then there's this." The taller Chechen said, setting the briefcase on a table to open the lid. The boss wandered over.

"Books?"

He looked at Stiletto.

"Care to explain yourself?"

Stiletto glared.

"Where is the uranium we agreed to buy?" the boss continued. "Are you trying to rip us off?" He came over to Stiletto and kicked him in the stomach. Stiletto doubled up, groaning and gasping some more. More fire in the belly, more pain spreading throughout. Stiletto opened his mouth wide to suck air.

"Tell us where it is, and we won't kill you."

Stiletto spat on the boss's left shoe.

The boss gestured to Shorty, who jammed the Colt in his belt and took out the ViperTek taser.

"Only a short burst," the boss said. "I don't want him unconscious."

Shorty grinned as he pressed the button and jabbed Stiletto in the leg once again. Stiletto choked, thrashing a little, overdoing it to work on the duct tape some more, spasms shaking his body. When the spasms stopped, he laid there, catching his breath. The ceiling above was quite black, lights hanging down, and speakers, too. He'd never seen the ceiling of a nightclub before and wondered why he found the sight so fascinating at this moment.

"Feel like talking now?"

"There's some chewing gum on the ceiling," Stiletto said.

"Boss," said the taller Chechen, coming over to the leader with his cell phone held out. "I uploaded his face to see if anybody knew who he was."

The boss looked at the phone's screen and raised an eyebrow.

"So, Mr. Stiletto. The Russians want to have a little chat with you, I see."

"They'll kill you rather than pay you."

"Wouldn't it be interesting to find out? Tell us where the uranium is, and we won't hand you over to them. Continue to get smart with me, and you'll be in Moscow by morning."

"Why not? Weather's better," Stiletto said. "Can you believe this humidity?"

The boss's face turned from neutral to angry, his brow

creasing and his lips in a flat line. He gestured at Shorty. "Full blast this time."

Shorty grinned again as he activated the ViperTek and aimed the prongs at Stiletto's stomach. The bolt of electricity snapped wildly between the prongs and Stiletto gave one last tug on the duct tape holding his wrists.

A little closer. . .

The duct tape ripped sharply, but the crackling taser covered the noise. Stiletto's left hand snapped out, grabbing Shorty's hand and shoving the taser back at him. He didn't make a full connection, but he made enough of one so that Shorty felt the jolt of electricity and bounced away from Stiletto. As he fell back, Stiletto's right hand grabbed for the .45 sticking out of his belt. Round in the chamber, finger on the trigger, Stiletto fired twice, blasting Shorty from aorta to heart, the blood spatter from the exit wounds slapping the dance floor.

Stiletto swung the Colt on the boss, firing as the man ran for cover. None of the rounds connected. Scott scrambled to his feet, only to feel the heavy boot of the tall Chechen smack into his belly. He doubled over once again, letting out a yell, ineffectually blocking the next blow that landed on the side of his head.

Stiletto pitched over, landing hard on the tile once again, rolling some more to get some distance. His hand still gripped the Colt, and as the Chechen closed in to kick the gun away, he found his forward moment stopped by an exploding knee cap. Stiletto raised his aim and fired another round into the man's head. He dashed out of the way as the tall Chechen's body fell face-first on the dance floor.

A pistol cracked, splitting the air above Scott. He stayed low, scrambling for a pair of large speakers off the dance floor. Through the gap between them, he watched Boss Man run from the console he'd been working on to the table area. Scott fired once and glass shattered behind the bar as Boss Man passed it.

Stiletto jumped from cover, careful to avoid the blood on the dance floor. He didn't need a slip-and-fall to add to his already bruised body. With his gun in a two-hand hold, Stiletto braced against a chair and fired twice. Boss Man was heading for the door. One of Stiletto's rounds nicked him in the left thigh, and he tumbled to the floor.

Scott wove through the tables as Boss Man fired back, rounds zipping by. Stiletto couldn't get a clear shot at him. Between the tables and raised chairs, the sitting area was surrounded by a small wall that divided it from the front, and Boss Man was down behind it. Stiletto aimed for the gap patrons passed through. He could hear Boss Man grunting as he crawled.

Stiletto stepped through the gap, leveling his gun on Boss Man, who winged a shot at him that flew wide. Stiletto fired twice. Flame spat from the muzzle of the pistol, the hot .45 ACP Hydra-Shok hollow-points tearing through the man's back, opening big holes on his front side and pinning him to the floor. Boss Man died with his eyes open.

But it didn't look like Boss Man had truly been heading for the door. Based on where his body pointed, it looked to Stiletto like he had been heading toward a door marked Private near the entrance. His office? Stiletto opened the door. Cluttered desk, posters on the wall, and various items, including a German MP-40 mounted on the wall behind the desk. Stiletto took the weapon off the display pegs and hefted it, checking the action and magazine. Yup, loaded with 9mm stingers. Boss Man had been going for heavy artillery, not the easy escape route.

Stiletto put the weapon back on the wall and snatched a set of keys from the desktop. The fob bore the familiar BMW logo, and Stiletto exited the club to find the silver sedan in the parking lot.

Waiting for him.

Scott put away his gun and dropped behind the wheel. Might as well drive in style back to the McDonald's to retrieve his rental.

He turned on the A/C full blast.

CHAPTER TWO

Paris.

Home.

Such as it was.

A long soak in the tub was what Stiletto required. The flight back from Rome had been quite crowded and bouncy from too much turbulence, a silent commentary on the mission that Stiletto preferred not to ponder.

After changing clothes at his hotel, where he also returned the rental car, Scott had sat quietly on the plane in a daze. He hurt all over, his gut especially tender to the touch, but it was the price he paid for a successful operation. At least as long as the Italian agency had collected the uranium. Perhaps that had been a little sloppy, but the Italians wouldn't waste time dealing with the tip he'd provided.

Stiletto leaned back in the tub and stared at the ceiling, letting the warm water take away the aches and pains. There was no chewing gum on his ceiling; the white paint was quite fresh, along with the paint in the rest of the place. His clothes were in a pile on the floor, and when his cell phone, which was somewhere in the pocket of his jeans, rang, he cursed. Leaning over the edge of the tub, dripping on the tiled floor, he grabbed a pant leg and pulled the jeans closer. He wiped his left hand on the denim and grabbed the cell phone. The number showed an Italian area code. Stiletto grinned.

"Yes," he answered.

"You took a big chance, Scott."

Stiletto smiled. "Stefano. How are you?"

"I am well," said Stefano Mortelli, a contact Stiletto knew from Italy's AISI. They weren't friends but had worked together once in the past.

Stiletto asked, "So you got my Valentine?"

"Who was on the other end?"

"You might have heard about a shooting in a night-club, sorry I didn't get the name."

"We found it. You probably already know about the Chechen ownership."

"That's a fine way of putting it."

"Well, among the bodies, we found a stash of drugs. Cocaine, pills, etcetera. It was a fully-functional night-club, but they sold more than booze at the bar."

"Sounds like I did you all a favor."

"Thank you for the effort."

"Trying to help. Maybe you can dig a little more and find out who brought the stuff there to begin with."

"We are certainly interested. Might you be free if we find something requiring your special skills?"

"Try me. You never know."

"Perhaps I'll be in touch."

"So long, Stefano."

Stiletto ended the call and dropped the cell on top of his clothes. He leaned back in the tub with a satisfied smile, but that didn't last long. A sudden ache removed the smile, and he groaned instead. He sank farther under the water.

The job had cost him not only physically, but monetarily too, since he'd paid his own freight. Given what he'd learned about the sale and the buyers, he couldn't let the Red Brigade and the Chechens make a deal, and passing the information along might not have guaranteed the successful interception of the uranium. It was an example of Stiletto's passion for protecting those who couldn't protect themselves. As awful as his situation might have been with the loss of his family, his CIA job, and all that, Stiletto at least found a small amount of solace in keeping other people from experiencing worse circumstances than his.

With those thoughts in mind, he dozed off in the tub.

Stiletto was watching the liver and onions sizzle when the phone rang.

He yanked the cell from his shirt pocket. Another number he recognized, but not one based in Italy. He answered.

"Hi, Suzi."

"Are you done," she said, "with your freebie job

wherein neither of us gets any money?"

Suzi Weber was Stiletto's go-between with potential clients. With him always on the road, she provided a fixed point of contact. She funneled jobs to various other freelancers as well, so those looking for a certain type of operator often checked with her first. She took a cut of the money from the job for compensation. Stiletto had no problem writing the checks.

A former CIA agent herself, Suzi had served in many hot zones, although now she was confined to a wheelchair after losing the use of her legs in a terrorist attack.

Suzi had been an analyst for the CIA in her past life and had worked with a team in Iraq during Operation Enduring Freedom. The team had used a small grocery store for cover, the store up front and fully operational, the agency personnel in the rear carrying out their mission. Insurgents found the hideout thanks to sloppy security from their team leader, who somehow gave away the location by not following proper tradecraft. Insurgents crashed a truckload of explosives through the store, the truck stopping in the center of a shopping aisle. The driver then touched off his bombs.

Six of her colleagues had died. She'd been lucky. Almost.

"All you think about is money," Stiletto said.

"I need shoes."

"Like you need a hole in the head."

"You're not funny."

"Sure I am. You're laughing on the inside. What's happening?"

"You're needed," Suzi said.

"Who's the client?"

"The fellow you call Number One. And it's not a request. Time to earn that stipend they pay you every month."

"He calls himself that. I didn't give him the name."

Stiletto was always ready for the old man's call. Number One was the man in charge of an organization called The Trust, made up of former intelligence officials who still wanted to fight the good fight, but without the red tape that blocked so many of those efforts within official governments. Stiletto didn't know the man's real name, but he had agreed to work for Number One on an as-needed basis after he had bailed Scott out of some serious trouble during the Russia fiasco.

"Where and when?"

Suzi gave him the location of a sidewalk café where a car would collect Stiletto at ten o'clock the next morning.

"I'll be there," he said.

Stiletto arrived at the Café Claude at 9:30 and ordered a cup of Earl Gray. Now he had a real elixir. Tea was far better than coffee, especially the rich Earl Gray to which Stiletto treated himself as every new day started.

It was a normal morning in Paris. Horns honked as traffic jammed in front of the café, pedestrians walking briskly on the sidewalk, one or two taking a side trip into the café while others continued past. Stiletto killed time by reading the news on his cell phone. The world was in its usual state of despair. After catching up on headlines, Stiletto redirected to a website where he could read some comic strips and enjoyed a chuckle or two. Noting the smudges on the touch-screen, he made a mental note to clean the surface later.

When a black limousine pulled up in front of the café, Stiletto put his phone away and grabbed his takeaway cup. As soon as he reached the back passenger door, it opened. He slipped inside. The limo merged with traffic before he had the door shut.

"Good morning," said Number One.

The old man sat across from Scott, the leather seats within as comfortable as his couch at home.

"I hear you've been busy," the old man continued.

Stiletto smiled. "Word gets around fast."

"The Italians have a lead on the source of the uranium," Number One said, "so they will have that case wrapped up shortly."

"I hope so. I told them I might be around if they needed me."

"You'll be busy."

"Is that a prediction?"

"More like a promise. We have a problem to solve in Venezuela."

"Since when, of late, have we not had problems to solve in Venezuela?"

The old man ignored the joke. "The US has been supporting the rebel army fighting to overthrow Lazaro Minas. They stepped up the effort after learning Minas wants to make the country a criminal sanctuary: a connection for drug traffic, human traffic, and other things. Minas needs new sources of investment now that the Russians have pulled out. Meanwhile, he maintains control over the population with death squads and work camps. Dissent is not tolerated."

"A hurricane hit there recently," Stiletto said. "Right?"

"Correct. Minas is in New York City to make a speech to the United Nations about sending hurricane relief. It will be quite the show."

"Problem is, the UN will swallow any lie he wants to tell. Dictators like him are very good at hiding their peoples' suffering."

"His speech isn't our concern right now. The rebels need guns and medicine. Your mission is to fly those items into the country and deliver them to the rebel forces."

"And then what? You wouldn't have brought me in only for a delivery."

"The CIA sent a team to train and advise the rebels."

"Oh, no."

"Oh, yes. They've been captured. We got the call because if word gets out, it could cause problems. Diplomatic problems; you know the kind. Your job is to break them out of a prison nobody has ever escaped from."

"Nobody?"

"Nobody who has also survived the shark-infested water surrounding the prison."

"Sounds like fun," Stiletto said.

"Two heads are better than one," Number One said, "so you'll have help. One of our newer operatives, Beth Carrington, will join you in Miami."

"What's in Miami?"

"The headquarters of an organization dedicated to sending relief and support to Venezuela."

"A front?"

"It is a Trust organization, yes. All good and proper. They're holding a fundraiser for hurricane relief, so the money is allegedly going to provide aid. We'll pay for more guns and medicine to ship at a later date, so in a way, we aren't lying to anybody."

Stiletto smiled. Duplicity was part of the spy business.

"I want you and Beth to attend the event to build your cover. If you're detained in Venezuela, you can fall back on the relief group."

Stiletto laughed. "That'll help. I get the idea the guy in charge won't care much who we represent."

"Best we can do on such short notice, but since Venezuela is also asking the UN for humanitarian aid, it makes sense. They won't want to mess with anybody bringing supplies into the country, and they'll especially want to keep quiet once UN inspectors show up to make sure the supplies are properly distributed."

Stiletto sipped his tea. "But why The Trust? Sounds

like the CIA already has an investment in the area."

"Once word of the capture reached us, we volunteered to help since we're going to be there anyway," Number One explained.

"That simple, huh?"

Number One shrugged. It was never that simple, as badly as the intelligence community would like such situations to be.

"Should I take the opportunity to remove this dictator if such an opportunity comes my way?"

"We won't be upset if that happened, no. But we also don't expect it to happen. It would be better for Venezuela if Americans were not involved in the fighting."

"It will be better for the United States if Americans aren't involved in the fighting," Stiletto said. "The last thing the public will support is another war."

Number One nodded. "In the meantime, book the next flight to Miami. Carrington will intercept you at your hotel."

"That's fine."

Stiletto didn't ask how Beth Carrington would find him. Number One had people everywhere. They'd know where Stiletto was before he did.

The man's introduction on their first meeting on a cold Moscow night several months ago had been direct and to the point.

"We're a group of retired intelligence professionals who unfortunately know the failings of the organized intelligence community. We formed The Trust to act in ways as the bureaucracies cannot. We have a cadre of operatives all over the world, in every country. You cannot go anywhere and not have a friend, if you know what I mean."

The Trust had wanted Stiletto to join their ranks as a full-time agent, but Scott had refused. He wanted to try the freelance life but said he'd be available if The Trust ever needed him.

They needed him now.

And Stiletto couldn't say no.

"How are you holding up overall?"

Stiletto blinked. He hadn't expected the question.

"I get by."

"You've had a hard time adjusting, I know," the old man said. "I faced the same difficulty when I retired. It was one of the reasons I formed The Trust. This work is in our blood. We'll never be able to turn it off."

Stiletto didn't reply, but Number One's fatherly tone meant a great deal. Suddenly he didn't feel like another anonymous freelancer. He wondered if he should accept the old man's offer of full-time employment after all.

"The Russians have been relentless," Number One said. "If you were to join us as a regular, we might be able to take the heat off."

He can read minds, apparently. "That's tempting."

"Keep it in mind. Think it over while you're in Venezuela."

"I will."

Number One lifted a handset from the door to his left and spoke to the driver. The limo pulled over.

"Right outside your apartment," Number One said.

Stiletto reached for the door handle on his side. "What don't you think of?"

He exited the limo with a quick good-bye and closed the door gently. The big car pulled away once again.

Stiletto went up to his apartment to pack.

Miami, Florida

Sal Parras drove slowly past the black Jaguar F-Type nestled in the third-level parking space between a Land Rover and a Volkswagen. Stiletto and the woman were still at the fund-raiser. Parras followed the arrows to the exit and parked illegally in a corner with a clear view of the entrance and exit gates.

He used his cell phone to examine the pictures of his targets once again, then set the phone aside to pull an FN-509 automatic pistol from under his suit jacket, to which he screwed a suppressor to the threaded end of the extended barrel.

Parras turned on some soft jazz and sat back to wait.

Shouldn't be long. Stiletto and the woman had a plane to catch within the hour. The boss's source, always trustworthy, had been certain of their agenda. Parras had wanted to ambush the pair when they reached the plane—

the plane with the medicine and weapons aboard—but the boss had nixed the idea. The Americans would cancel the flight when Stiletto and the woman failed to show. Keeping the plane from leaving the US was the goal, and if Parras somehow missed, he couldn't shoot down the plane without a support team and heavy weapons. That kind of operation and its associated logistics was something El Presidente wanted to avoid.

Parras was part of El Presidente's personal death squad. He had been sent from the Central American nation to deal with the two Americans who were bringing more death and destruction to a nation that had already seen its fair share. In recent months, the Americans had seen fit to interfere with Venezuela, which didn't make sense to Parras. The only people imprisoned or put to death by El Presidente were criminals, like the rebels. Why would the Americans care about them?

Parras also knew, as he sat in the garage waiting for his targets, that his beloved El Presidente was in New York City, about to make a speech at the United Nations. Among other things, he was going to deny the allegations against him. He was no murderer. He was a kind leader who knew what was best for his people even if they did not understand his wisdom.

Parras hadn't been in the US long, and he wouldn't be staying after the hit, either. He had his own plane to catch, a private charter that would return him to Caracas in time for breakfast.

"You don't look like you're having a good time, Mr. Stiletto."

Scott Stiletto raised an eyebrow at the woman before him. She wore a sequined strapless party dress that sparkled. She had to look up at him. She couldn't have been more than 5'6."

Stiletto sipped his martini—gin, not vodka. If he had one wish, he'd go back in time and smack some sense into the English gent who had popularized the so-called "vodka martini."

He wasn't sure what to tell her. He didn't know if she knew anything about his background, and he certainly wasn't going to tell his life story when they were supposed to be playing a role.

Being back in the US reminded him of his old life and the people he'd left behind.

"I'm okay," he said instead. "Been a busy few days."

"The boss told me you mostly work on your own."

"That's right."

They paused awkwardly.

"I do think it's funny, actually," he said, "that this fundraiser is full of con men hired by you-know-who."

"This is a charity ball, not a swindle."

"I think you believe the cover story a little too much."

"The money will go to Venezuela one way or another."

"The money will pay for a truckload of guns, for sure."

She scowled.

"Beth, come on. The people who show up to parties like this pull out their best clothes and jewelry and get their egos fed by the pitchmen who talk about starving kids and lack of medicine and how they alone can change the world, and the suckers get so worked up, they try to top each other for who can write the biggest check. Scams work the same way—same techniques. There's always somebody ready to contribute to your cause or invest in your product. They only need to hear the right story."

He glanced at the woman, who suddenly had nothing to say.

She wasn't unattractive, with the trim figure one expected from a covert operative, her hair short enough to remain out of the way but long enough to tie back, as she wore it now. Her blue eyes stood out against her otherwise pale white skin, framed by dark eyebrows that set off the red lipstick on her small mouth.

"I'm not sure how to respond, Mr. Stiletto."

"Play your role, and we'll be fine." Stiletto tossed back the remains of his martini and handed her the glass. She took it without thinking. "Get me a refill?"

"I don't think you're very funny, Mr. Stiletto."

"Call me Scott."

She left him with a glare.

Stiletto scanned the dancing crowd and looked at all the shiny jewelry available and thought it might be nice to lift one or two items to see if he still had the touch—not that he used it much. Talent fades without practice. The CIA taught case officers how to pick pockets same as they taught them how to pick locks. One never knew when grabbing somebody's wallet would reveal a clue that might prevent an international disaster, and Stiletto knew of at least two cases where major problems had been prevented by such small efforts.

The fundraiser had been going on for a couple of hours, so everybody was properly liquored, and still parading in front of each other like a bunch of cocks showing off their bright feathers. If the necklaces posed a challenge, there were always gold bracelets, diamond rings, and expensive gold Rolexes up for grabs. All he'd have to do was pull one of the single ladies onto the dance floor for a spin and deprive her of grandma's rings. A chat with some of the gentleman, with assorted "good ol' boy" jokes that always worked, and he'd have a pocket full of Rolexes with which to waltz out. He wouldn't have to take another freelance job for a few months or even a year if he correctly budgeted the money received for the fenced items.

Stop it! He shook his head in disgust. This wasn't any way to behave, and maybe he'd been too harsh with Beth. He hadn't meant to be. The black tuxedo he wore annoyed him. His skin itched under the white shirt, and the bow tie was a little too tight around his neck.

But those were excuses, he knew. What Number One had said about The Life being in his DNA bothered him. "This work is in our blood. We'll never be able to turn it off." Stiletto had to admit it was true. There was no way out for people like them.

Any semblance of a normal life had gone through the rock crusher already, his own family, to start. Then there had been an old flame in San Francisco who'd had the idea they could start again—Ali Lewis. And what about Kim Jordan in Seattle? He'd said good-bye to her after two otherwise blissful weeks. He couldn't stay in one place too long. He always had to be moving, leaving personal disaster in his wake.

There was also Nikki Fortune in Italy, the wild child of a genuine Italian gangster who was always looking for a quick way to get rich and falling flat on her face as she did so. Maybe the best choice was to find somebody exactly like him and call it a day.

How do you turn all that off? How do you start over?

Stiletto had no idea. There weren't exactly any career counselors he could talk to.

"What transferrable skills do I bring to the private sector?"

"What did you do before, sir?"

"Killed bad guys and blew up stuff."

"Have you considered teaching kindergarten?"

Ridiculous.

As he scanned the dance floor and wondered where Beth Carrington had gone with his drink, Stiletto's doubts about her grew. Number One had said she was new to the team, and while he rated her highly, Stiletto still needed proof she was as capable as the old man said before he would trust her with his life. Maybe a peace offering would help thaw the ice, and they could really get to know each other.

He certainly hadn't started out on the right foot.

He pulled at the bow tie to lessen the pressure on his neck, but the relief was short-lived. Next time he wore a bow tie, he'd make it a little looser and to hell with whether it looked proper or not.

Scott cursed under his breath.

Beth Carrington waited while the bartender mixed Stiletto's martini. Why had she taken the glass? She couldn't figure that out. She should have told him to get his own drink, but at that moment, she'd had no power to say no. Had he pulled some sort of mind trick on her? At least it gave her an excuse to get away from him. The bartender placed the glass in front of her. She ordered a red wine for herself. Why not? She needed it. The bartender quickly filled another glass. With both in hand, she turned from the bar and proceeded through the crowd.

She didn't know what to think of Stiletto. All Number One had said was that he was a special asset called in for the operation, and his responsibilities weren't for her to worry about.

She had wanted to enjoy the ball and fundraiser. The Trust, in setting up Relief for Venezuela, certainly hadn't missed any detail.

Her personal stake in the mission was that she hated

to see women and children being abused. Venezuela's dictator didn't care who was on the other end of his death squad's guns. Women and children were also fair game, like the men who opposed the nation's "great leader," Lazaro Minas.

It made Beth sick. Minas was the kind of man who needed to be hung from a lamp post in the public square, his body desecrated by the survivors of his murder crew.

If there was any trouble with the Venezuelan authorities along the way, they could claim they were on a humanitarian mission. That was the plan, anyway. There were some genuine medical supplies waiting for her and Stiletto on the DC-10, but the small arms were stashed underneath. Her job was to make sure the guns reached the rebels and that they knew how to use them.

Beth Carrington had grown up in New Hampshire, the middle child of a well-connected and wealthy family, the members of which had served a variety of presidential administrations. She had a high sense of right and wrong and patriotism, all the ingredients the CIA liked, but she'd failed the entry exams and missed out on an analyst job at CIA headquarters. Unsure of what she'd do next in her life, she drifted through a few odd jobs, and then a nice old man who refused to give his name but called himself "Number One" had paid a visit to her family's home while she was visiting one weekend. The man and her father knew each other well enough, it seemed. He asked for a private meeting with Beth and gave her his pitch. Join The Trust, he said. We're like the CIA, but not as disorganized, and we do good work around the world. She'd said OK. After a period of acclimation and getting to know other Trust operatives, she'd begun getting her own assignments, quickly establishing herself as a tough and resourceful operative who could be counted on.

The Trust wanted capable idealists. The kind who wouldn't ask too many questions as long as they were fighting for the red, white, and blue, ideals that had been instilled in Beth Carrington from birth. It was the perfect match. And they paid better than the CIA anyway.

So why had she been paired with grumpy Scott Stiletto, who thought the fundraiser resembled a criminal conspiracy of con men fleecing marks? Why not one of the other qualified agents she knew well and who shared her point of view?

Her intuition told her Stiletto wasn't all that he seemed.

She would have to exercise some patience.

Good luck with that.

She wove around an older couple, lifting the drinks high to avoid spillage, and rejoined Stiletto.

He took the offered martini and said thank you.

"You're lucky I didn't spit in it," she said.

"Wouldn't have mattered."

"Oh?"

"It's alcohol." He took a long drink. She glared at him.

"I don't think we're going to get along, Scott."

"By the time this mission is over, we'll be great friends."

"I doubt it."

"Wanna bet?"

He winked.

Now she really hated him.

"Don't take too long with that," he said, gesturing at her wine. "We need to leave soon."

She glanced at the small watch on her thin wrist. He was right. She took a long swallow. Maybe if she were a little buzzed, she could tolerate him better.

Beth Carrington screamed as she fell headlong onto the hard concrete of the garage. Stiletto landed on top of her. The rapid spits of a suppressed pistol echoed in the garage's confines.

Stiletto grabbed her by the arm and hauled her up. Her tight-fitting sequined party dress was in disarray, but there wasn't time to adjust it. Stiletto urged her ahead, and she ran. Stiletto looked back. The assassin rounded the aisle and stopped to aim his pistol.

Stiletto carried no weapon this time. His gear was waiting for him on the DC-10. Who expected a gunfight at a simple fundraiser?

He wasn't sure if Beth was armed, but he hoped she had something stashed under her skirt. He stayed low, and the assassin fired. The shot whined off the roof of a car. Stiletto ran after Beth, the bottom edge of his tuxedo jacket flapping, his formerly shiny dress shoes now scuffed and dirty in their own right.

"Turn left!" he shouted. "Left!"

She followed his direction, squeezing between two cars. Stiletto bumped his elbow on a side mirror and stifled a grunt as pain flashed through his arm. Beth almost passed the black Jaguar F-Type Stiletto had acquired for the night, but stopped and fumbled for the recessed door handle. No luck. Stiletto hit the key fob as he approached. The handle popped out, and she jumped in. He dropped behind the wheel and started the motor. Speeding out of the space, he aimed for the exit, racing down the aisle as the assassin blocked the way.

Beth pulled up her skirt and clawed for a compact Rock Island Armory CS Tactical 1911-A1 .45 auto in a garter holster. Perfect. Stiletto powered down her window. She leaned out and fired four rapid shots, the unsuppressed cracks loud and thundering. The assassin dropped and rolled as the glare of the headlights bore down on him. Stiletto caught a brief glimpse of an angry face as the Jag thundered by.

That makes two of us, pal. We'll see each other again.

Stiletto steered the F-Type coupe out of the garage and turned left onto the nearly empty street. After blasting through a red light, he took a couple of sharp turns, Beth slamming against the passenger door.

"Buckle up," he said. "It's the law."

Beth quickly snapped the seat belt in place. With a sigh, she tugged on her dress and wiped at an oil stain.

"This outfit is ruined."

"You're alive."

"The old man didn't mention anything about the other side sending an assassin after us!"

"It means," Stiletto said, "somebody on our side talked."

"Are you serious?"

"How else do you explain what happened?"

"We have to call The Trust!"

"Let's get to the plane first."

"But if they knew we were at the fundraiser, they'll know about the airstrip!" she said.

"Stop yelling," he replied. "I'm counting on it."

"You're insane. You have no idea how to handle this kind of situation."

Stiletto laughed.

"It's not funny!"

"The airstrip is surrounded by security people armed with automatic weapons. The bad guys sent one man to kill us. Do you really think he'll have a chance against our crew?"

Beth said nothing more.

Stiletto focused on the road. A dirty job.

Number One hadn't minced words about what he and Beth Carrington were expected to accomplish.

He didn't know what to expect as they ventured forward, but he had to admit the challenge had brought some excitement. He couldn't wait to see the infamous prison in which the CIA team was being held. He couldn't wait to be the man to break other men out of said prison.

The Jag thundered through traffic.

Sal Parras, breathing heavily, returned to his car. He dropped the FN-509 on the passenger seat. Smoke still trickled from the muzzle, and the scent of cordite tickled his nose.

He drove out of the garage. He'd seen Stiletto and the woman turn left, and he followed. The black Jaguar shouldn't be too hard to catch up with. He had a fast car, too. He powered ahead, the engine of the turbo Audi growling under direct injection. So much for the boss's bright idea. Parras should have followed his instincts and ambushed the pair at the airstrip, and taken out the plane at the same time.

But there was still time to salvage the mission.

CHAPTER THREE

"Slow down, or we'll get a ticket," said Beth Carrington.

They were crossing the MacArthur Causeway, leaving Miami Beach behind. Stiletto wove in and out of lanes, other cars mere flashes as they rocketed by, the Jag's supercharged engine pumping out the commanded horsepower.

"He's behind us," Stiletto said.

"What?"

Beth raised herself and twisted around in the seat, shifting the shoulder belt away to look out the back window.

"Where is he?"

"Back there."

"I can't tell one from the other."

"Trust me, Beth. He's catching up."

"I think I got him."

"See?"

She dropped back into the seat and checked the magazine in her CS Tactical .45 auto. "I only have four rounds left."

"We can't have a gunfight in the middle of Miami," Stiletto told her.

"Why not? Everybody will think we're drug dealers or something."

Stiletto laughed. "Sounds like one of my lines."

"What's your plan, Scott?"

Stiletto swung into the right lane, lifting off the gas and downshifting the six-speed gearbox to slow the car. He took the next exit at speed, tires screeching on the tight curve of the cloverleaf. Once off the exit, he hit the gas again.

Stiletto snapped his eyes to the rearview mirror. The assassin's car was still back there. Plenty of drivers had an Audi on the road, but only one stayed on Stiletto's back, matching his speed and movements, trying to catch up.

A blur of city streets followed Stiletto's sudden turns as he avoided stoplights by turning onto side streets. Too many homes. Apartments. Shopping areas. Places where witnesses could see them. He needed a location where nobody was around. The last thing he needed was somebody capturing a fight on a cell phone camera. They might still make it to the airstrip outside the city, but not with an APB out for the Jag and the two people inside.

"Right there!" Beth said, pointing.

"Excellent idea," Stiletto agreed. He swung the Jaguar right, into the parking lot of a school. No lights were on in any of the buildings, the campus mostly dark except for walkway lights here and there. Stiletto stopped the Jag outside a building and he and Beth jumped out. A racing engine grew louder, proving he hadn't been wrong. The assassin had stuck, and had probably seen the turn.

Stiletto ran, his dress shoes tapping hard on the concrete. Beth followed, her bare feet slapping the ground, and she cried out as she stepped on a rock. She kept up with him as he rounded the corner of the building and flattened himself against the textured wall.

Breathing hard, she raised her gun.

Stiletto put a hand on her wrist, shaking his head. She lowered the gun, holding it close to her leg.

The assassin pulled into the parking lot. Tires screeched, then a door opened but didn't close. The engine remained running.

Stiletto looked at Beth and put a finger to his lips. She nodded.

He waited. The assassin wore soft-soled shoes, but they still made noise on the concrete. One of the walkway lights caught a shadow, and it moved across the ground slowly. Then it stopped. The assassin knew as well as Stiletto that the light betrayed his position, and the killer didn't know where his quarry was.

Beth breathed quietly beside him. His kingdom for a suppressor on her .45!

Shoes scraped. Footsteps. Going the other way.

Stiletto raced around the corner, bent at the waist, aiming his tackle for the assassin's back.

The killer turned, bringing up his pistol. Stiletto connected solidly with his midsection, a rush of air leaving the killer's lungs as his feet left the ground. They flew back, landing in a clump of bushes, Stiletto going for the killer's neck with both hands.

The assassin's hot eyes locked on Stiletto's face, his hands coming up to block Scott's, a punch following. Stiletto lifted his left elbow, deflecting the blow, hammering his right fist into the killer's face once, twice. The assassin still clutched his FN pistol and he swung it at Stiletto, Scott grabbing for the gun with both hands. Doing so exposed him, and the killer used his free hand to land hard blows on Stiletto's face. Scott winced as he rolled and pulled the killer's hand with him, the assassin crying out as his hand bent with the roll and his trigger finger snapped. The FN slipped into Stiletto's grip.

Scott sat up, swinging hard. The steel barrel of the FN pistol hit the assassin with a solid smack. The assassin looked surprised as his head fell back, the rest of his body flattening as he fell. Out cold. Stiletto jumped to his feet, bits of leaves and branches stuck to his tuxedo. He staggered back onto the concrete.

"Beth!"

She ran around the corner. He didn't need to tell her twice. They raced back to the Jag. Stiletto jumped behind the wheel and dropped the FN-509 in the footwell near Beth's feet. He powered backward, swinging around the still-running Audi and back onto the street.

He drove slower this time, steering through the housing tract as his breathing returned to normal.

Beth said, "Are you hurt?"

"Might have a bruise or two," he said. "This tux is finished. Not that I was going to keep it anyway."

"At least he won't follow us to the airstrip."

"But you can bet the enemy knows we're coming," he said. "This mission is already compromised."

"Do we abort?"

"Nobody tries to kill me and lives to make a second attempt," Stiletto assured her.

She made no reply.

The bright headlamps of the Jag F-Type cut through the narrow roadway as Stiletto steered along the dirt road, presently stopping at a closed gate. He hopped out long enough to push the gate open, from which the lock had already been removed, and drove the Jag through.

The forest on either side, in the night time darkness, held plenty of critters but hopefully no two-legged threats. Stiletto kept his eyes open anyway after what had happened in the garage, and he noted that Beth Carrington kept her index finger outside the trigger guard of her Rock Island .45.

The only people with guns Stiletto wanted to see was the security crew around the plane, the ones sent by Number One and The Trust to make sure they lifted off safely.

And that was exactly what Scott Stiletto saw once they entered a clearing where a DC-10 sat on a makeshift runway along with at least ten armed men with automatic rifles and full body armor.

Stiletto stopped the Jag as one of the guards approached the car.

"Good evening, sir," the guard said. "I'm Matheson. Your plane is ready, and the gear is aboard."

"Any trouble?" Stiletto said, rising from the car.

"Nothing at all. Why?"

Stiletto laughed a little. Beth came around the front. She still clutched her pistol.

"You can put that away now," Stiletto told her.

"Yeah, right."

Matheson said, "Follow me."

Stiletto looked around as Matheson led him and Beth to the plane. The guards stood well apart from each other around the perimeter of the airstrip. They climbed a set of steps into the cabin, lit by a line of lights on either side of the interior. The canvas seats with their steel-frame backs didn't look very comfortable.

Up near the cockpit, were a stack of wooden crates, perhaps eight in total. All showed various stamps and markings to appear legitimate, but Stiletto knew the crates held automatic weapons, pistols, ammunition, and explosive ordnance for the Venezuelan rebels at war with a brutal dictator trying curry favor with the United Nations.

Stiletto feared that Minas' veneer of respectability would fool the UN and they'd give him everything he wanted.

It had happened many times before.

Stiletto checked the back of the plane, where he found their backpacks containing personal supplies, clothes, and other items. A quick search revealed Stiletto's pistol and spare ammunition, secured and ready for action. Beth accounted for her own gear and spare clothing. Stiletto, awkwardly, because the corners snagged on the fabric of the pack, pulled out a wooden box.

"All set?"

Beth shook her head and found a seat.

Matheson wished them a safe trip, folded the steps into the plane and shut the fuselage door. The twin props rumbled to life. Stiletto sat and bucked his lap belt. The DC-10 bounced a little as it moved down the runway, picking up speed, and when he felt the familiar lurch in his stomach, Stiletto knew they were airborne.

The steel frame of the seat dug into Stiletto's back and pressed into his legs. Nice. A twelve-hour flight in a seat like this. Well, he'd suffered through worse. A glance at Beth Carrington, though, and the frown on her face, followed by the occasional wince as the plane hit turbulence, showed she would not be having a good time at all.

Stiletto glanced at the wooden box he held. In it was some food he'd brought to help pass the time. It was all he had for a peace offering with Beth Carrington, but he wondered if she even ate the kinds of snacks he'd packed—a brick of cheddar cheese and a summer sausage roll, along with some crackers and 20-year-old scotch. Glenfiddich, specifically. The box also contained a travel humidor with a few of his cigars.

Once the plane leveled off, Beth grabbed her bag, went into the bathroom at the rear to change, and emerged in jeans and a flannel shirt. Stiletto changed out of his tux as well, and when he returned to his seat, Beth said, "What's in the box?"

Stiletto smiled, flipped the catch, and raised the lid. "Some snacks. Cheese and crackers and summer sausage."

"Is that scotch?"

"Twenty-year Glenfiddich, yes."

"Quite fancy."

"It's a tough life," Stiletto said. "Might as well live it up when you can."

"Well, pass me some of those vitamins, and I'll join you."

Stiletto grabbed one of the two plastic cups in the box and poured scotch into it, then passed the cup to Beth. The turbulence bounced them around a little as he passed pieces of cheese and sausage to her.

Stiletto hoped they were on the road to being friends. Life could be tough, and it helped to have friends outside the line of fire.

Beth Carrington wondered if she'd misjudged Scott Stiletto.

How could a guy who liked good scotch and greasy

sausage be that bad? She'd have expected him to be a beer man, but she knew better than to refuse good scotch. Her father always had a bottle of Glenfiddich around during holidays and family gatherings in the Hamptons, so sipping the elixir, despite the fact that it was in a plastic cup she hadn't had the opportunity to rinse out, reminded her of home. That was never a bad thing. Her father would be very proud of her and what she was doing right now. Too bad she could never tell him, which was a way of life in the spy business. He'd at least understand the secrecy.

Stiletto unwrapped the cheese, then the summer sausage. It was beef, his preferred flavor over pork, he explained, and it was warm and properly greasy to the touch as he set it down in the box and wiped his hands on a cloth napkin.

"You like being shot at?" she said.

"Not particularly."

"Neither do I."

"You handled yourself well. The pistol was a nice touch. I'm glad you had it."

She smiled shyly.

He sliced the sausage and cheese and handed her a pile of each, along with a handful of crackers, on a small plate. Then he shifted in his seat to look out the window at the dark night. She glanced out her own window. Total darkness. You couldn't sense that the plane was moving.

She stared out the window into the black and wondered what was going to happen to her.

The sun shone on New York City.

Lazaro Minas stood in front of the large pane of glass that substituted for a wall in his hotel suite, allowing an extended view of the sprawling city and skyline laid out before him as if it were a newly conquered land. If only. His kingdom lay farther south.

Minas was short and stocky but carried himself proudly, his broad shoulders and chest giving him the appearance of strength while his carefully trimmed beard, always close to his skin, showed a man in quiet control.

Another man sat at a table to the right of Minas, furiously typing on a laptop. When the typing stopped, Minas said, "Read the last paragraph back to me."

The man, Minas' speechwriter, peered through the bifocals perched on his nose.

"'We ask that the UN approve the requested funds for humanitarian aid. Hurricane Margaret has decimated our nation. Our people are without homes and without their livelihoods, and are suffering greatly. A shortage of food and necessary goods threatens the lives of our people, including children. If necessary, we will welcome a UN commission to oversee the distribution of humanitarian aid, but we have a plan in place that should satisfy the committee that Venezuela can lift itself from the ashes of this tragedy and emerge a stronger nation.'"

Minas considered the words while watching yellow cabs on the street below. So many yellow cabs. They were like ants to him from the height of his hotel room.

"Very good," Minas said. "Print a copy, and I'll do a little practice and make some changes."

The speechwriter said okay and tapped two keys. A wireless printer that was also on the table hummed to life and pages began sliding into the catch tray.

"We should also," the speechwriter said, easing back from the table to cross his legs, "include material on the allegations of human rights abuses, sir."

"Absolutely," Minas agreed. "Those lies must be rebutted. While I'm practicing, draft whatever you see fit, but be sure to include that these allegations are lies from surrounding nations that do not wish to see Venezuela prosper. They want us weakened so they can ferment disruption and take our oil and gold."

"Yes, sir."

The speechwriter removed the pages from the tray once the printer stopped and brought them over to Minas. The President of Venezuela remained by the window and quietly started reading.

The door across the room opened, and Minas turned. One of the guards from the outer hall who carried a pistol on his belt said, "Excuse me, El Presidente, but you have a visitor. He says his name is Ramon Salazar and said to tell you, 'Morning Star.'"

"Show him in," Minas said. He folded the papers and shoved them into the left breast pocket of his suit coat. He dismissed the speechwriter as the guard showed Ramon Salazar into the suite. When the door closed, Minas smiled, held out his arms, and met Salazar in the middle of the room. The two men embraced and greeted each other warmly.

"How are you enjoying New York City?" Minas asked.

"It's noisy."

"Not from up here, it isn't," Minas said, laughing, and moved across the room to a mini bar. He poured two glasses of bourbon and handed one to Salazar as he gestured to a couch. The two men sat opposite each other.

Salazar sipped his drink. "This is good bourbon."

Minas nodded. He noted that Salazar wore a suit like his, similarly tailored. He wasn't sure he liked that. He couldn't have his subordinates looking as good or better than he did. Salazar already had looks in his corner. He was trimmer and better built than Minas, and taller versus Minas' rotund frame, but then Minas dismissed the thought. Salazar had his own responsibilities to attend to; he had to look the part, same as Minas.

Salazar was a critical component of an operation Minas had put in motion two weeks earlier. He wasn't going to jeopardize that over a suit. Or a body shape.

"Give me your update," Minas said.

"Parras failed in his assassination mission. I sent him home."

"That does not please me, Ramon."

"The plane with the guns and ammunition will be in the air by now," Salazar said. "Halfway to Venezuela."

"Your source in Zurich is sure of this?"

"We hacked their computers. Actual documents, notes, and coordinates don't lie."

"You're going back?"

"Yes, on the first evening flight. The charade must go on, and we might learn more that will help us."

"You like the girl, too?" Minas smiled.

Ramon Salazar grinned. "I don't dislike her, no. I also don't want her to suspect me. If I vanish on her, she might get ideas."

Minas sighed and looked at the amber fluid in his glass. Inside sources were hard to acquire and tougher to cultivate when they weren't aware of what they were being used for. Salazar had no choice but to return and continue the mission, albeit with the possibility he would remain only long enough to keep her from guessing his true agenda.

He said, "We cannot let the rebels get their hands on those guns or the token supply of medical equipment. I will alert the coastal radar stations. When the plane appears, we will blow it out of the sky. End of problem."

Salazar nodded.

"It was good to see you, my friend," Minas said, setting his glass on the coffee table.

Salazar took the hint and placed his unfinished drink on the table as well. They said good-bye, and Minas stood alone for a moment. He looked at the view of the city once again.

He hadn't wanted to take over the leadership of Venezuela, but circumstances had forced his hand. He didn't try to fight the circumstances very hard, though.

Minas had begun his career as a labor organizer, and the money was good, but he quickly realized through his dealings with politicians that they had all the comforts he was looking for—the cash, the women, the yes-men. He ran for and won a spot on the National Assembly, and soon rose in the ranks and became a popular champion of the working class, who had insisted he take over the presidential palace when his ailing predecessor finally died.

Up until then, he had quietly been socking away cash, preparing for the moment when he could leave Venezuela and afford to live anywhere in the world. He had acquired a wife during that time, and when the people had demanded his leadership, she had joined their voices. Minas declared his intent to replace the former president, and to make sure he won all the votes, had his minions stuff ballot boxes and intimidate those intending to vote for his challenger. Minas won the election, taking seventy percent of the vote, but soon the country began sinking into economic malaise, with rapid job loss, rising poverty, rampant crime, and general unpleasantness that gave rise to a rebel army that wanted him out of power.

Minas had responded by instituting welfare programs, nationalizing formerly private enterprises, and stamping out the rebel threat, which often included using lethal force against people known to be affiliated with the group, or even suspected. Those not killed went into work camps. The rebels had to understand that he wasn't a man to be trifled with.

Fighting the rebels had soon brought charges of human rights violations from the world outside, creating more problems.

Minas continued to insist that he treated his countrymen fairly, but there was always some group of do-gooders sneaking in to report the real story. He had a full staff of spokespeople to counter their statements, and another technical team dedicated to sniffing out illegal radio stations and messages on social media and snuffing out the problems at the source.

And then the Americans had sent a CIA team to help train the rebel army and supply weapons and equipment. The only saving grace of their arrival was that they couldn't very well tell anybody what they found on the ground because their mission was classified. The Americans only wanted access to Venezuela's natural resources. They would not have bothered had there been no gold or oil below the ground.

Taking out the papers on which his speech was printed, he stood in front of a wall mirror and worked on his facial expressions as he read the lines, pausing now and then to cross out lines and rewrite. Everything needed to look natural. He needed to win a Hollywood Oscar for his performance.

If the UN was going to agree to his request for humanitarian aid, he had to make sure they saw the side of him he wanted them to see and nothing else.

"Can you believe the stones on this punk?"

"Worse, the assembly is hanging on every word."

The two US State Department representatives watched Minas give his speech from an upper balcony in the UN General Assembly, his admittedly commanding presence at the podium backed up by two jumbo screens showing his face behind him. Midway through the speech, the screens played a video of happy and smiling people all over Venezuela, with some shots of hurricane damage and the rescue and clean-up efforts, some of those same people smiling as they rebuilt homes and cleared streets. Minas' point was that his country did not look like the kind of place where political opponents were jailed or killed.

"They're going to give him every cent he asks for," said one of the State Department men.

"Uh-huh. And he will divert every penny to his own pocket."

"This speech could be a comedy skit."

"But it's funny for the wrong reasons."

Much later, after a short debate, the UN General Assembly, including the United States, voted to provide Venezuela with money and relief assistance in the wake of the recent hurricane. Minas and his entourage beamed as El Presidente thanked the committee and made big promises about the use of the funds.

CHAPTER FOUR

When Stiletto finally woke up with a stiff back and a pain in his side from where the seat frame was beating on him, he heard Beth Carrington's voice.

"Right, he was waiting for us," she said.

Stiletto saw her talking on her cell phone, probably updating Number One about their rather dramatic exit from the parking garage.

Scott glanced out the window. Ocean, ocean, everywhere, and not a drop to drink. Clouds dotted the sky here and there. They were probably somewhere over the Caribbean Sea. Had they passed Cuba? He would have loved to stop in the Dominican Republic and visit some cigar factories, after a prior stop in Cuba to pick up some excellent rum. Stiletto didn't care for Cuban cigars. Habanos lived on its old reputation and their "forbidden fruit" aura in the United States, although with the recent lifting of import restrictions, more Americans had a chance to try Cuban cigars, albeit on a limited basis. Cigars from the

D.R., Honduras, and Nicaragua were much better. Stiletto knew better than to give that opinion to his fellow cigar nuts, however. GroupThink propagated by bull roars from smokers who didn't know any better and magazines like Cigar Aficionado demanded that one always, without fail, praise Cuban tobacco, no matter what.

He checked his watch and figured they had another two hours before entering Venezuelan air space. Hopefully.

He ignored the rest of Beth's conversation as he stood and stretched, then used the bathroom. By the time he emerged, she was off the phone and looking out the window.

"What did the boss say?"

Stiletto sat next to her, and she didn't flinch. Good. Maybe the ice between them was thawing after all. The scotch probably helped.

"He's going to investigate," she told him.

"Great." Stiletto blinked.

"Something on your mind?"

"Not sure how he's going to do that. Does The Trust have a headquarters or something?"

She raised an eyebrow. "Are you joking?"

"My only interaction has been with Number One. And now you, of course."

"The Trust has a small headquarters and staff," Beth said. "He'll start there and see if word of our mission got through a crack or something."

"Or something."

"They might be waiting for us, you know."

"True."

"You aren't nervous?"

"I've faced worse."

"I don't—"

"Hey." Stiletto jerked a thumb toward the crates up front. "We have plenty of guns, right?"

Beth Carrington shook her head.

The pilot announced they'd be landing within an hour, so Stiletto and Beth re-packed their personal gear and checked their weapons.

He'd already oiled the action on the Colt .45, and it moved slickly. Beth was right. If the enemy forces in Venezuela knew they were coming and were perhaps planning a reception after failing to take them out in the States, they had to be ready to deal with the problem the hard way. Stiletto secured the pistol in a shoulder holster, which he then wrapped around his torso and secured to his belt.

The DC-10 lurched suddenly, the nose pointing up. Stiletto, out of his seat, tumbled back. Beth screamed. Stiletto scrambled to the nearest seat, thankful the steel frame gave him something to hold onto. Out the window, he saw the long contrail of a missile as the heat-seeker corrected to come back at the DC-10, closing the distance at an alarming rate.

"Missile!" Stiletto shouted.

The DC-10 leveled out, then dipped left, the pilot putting the plane into a dive.

"Never mind them waiting for us!" Stiletto said. "They're trying to knock us out of the sky!"

The DC-10 began rocking back and forth, loud explosions detonating outside the plane. Puffs of black smoke showed through the window. Anti-aircraft fire. Loads of it, filling the sky. The pilot's evasive action swung the plane left and right, but eventually a louder boom sounded, the plane rocking hard, and flames began licking at the fuselage on Stiletto's side. He unstrapped from his seat and hopped across the aisle behind Beth before strapping in again.

"Are we hit?" she shouted.

The DC-10 dipped into a dive.

Beth said, "I'll take that as a yes!"

The lap belt dug painfully into Stiletto's midsection, and his vision shook with the vibration of the plane. He shut his eyes tight.

The assassin waiting in the garage and now this.

The Trust had a leak, and no mistake.

The mission might end before it began, but Stiletto hoped he lived long enough to find out who had betrayed them.

The downward pitch of the plane steepened. Scott occupied his chair with a sense of helplessness. The only thing keeping him in place was his lap strap. As the plane rocked and bounced in rapid descent, he didn't feel very secure at all.

The DC-10 left a spiraling trail of black smoke in the sky as it plunged toward the earth. Pilot and co-pilot finally managed to straighten out, but the anti-aircraft fire had not only struck the left engine, but penetrated the rear fuselage as well, including the rear elevators and part of the tail. The pilot had about half as much control of the plane as he needed. He managed to aim the plane at the widest open space below, which didn't look long enough. The terrain wasn't entirely flat, and the mass of trees around the perimeter spelled catastrophe if he couldn't stop the plane.

The DC-10 lurched down again, the nose coming back up a second later. Stiletto cursed. Why did it have to take so long to fall out of the sky?

Then there was a big boom as the plane touched down with such force that lap strap or not, Scott flew out of his seat, bounced off the ceiling, and landed flat on the floor. Beth Carrington screamed again. Loose items around the cabin flew like stray meteors, ricocheting around. Another thunderous crash with a sudden stop, and Stiletto lost his grip on consciousness. The lights went out.

Lazaro Minas could not wait to get back home.

He stepped out of the Lincoln SUV with his security entourage and made for the waiting Lear jet sitting on the airport tarmac. JFK was a busy airport, but the private hangar where the Lear had waited was well enough away from the main terminal that Minas and his crew remained undisturbed. Diplomatic immunity often proved useful. Once aboard the plane, Minas sat in a big leather chair, and the lone stewardess was waiting with a cold martini. His security team filed inside and took their seats. Somebody's cell phone rang. The bodyguard who answered spoke one word to the caller and handed his phone to Minas.

"Home, sir," he said.

Minas took the phone. "Yes?"

"The plane with the supplies and guns," said Minas' number two, General Vitorio Florez, "has been shot down."

"Survivors?"

"A team is on the way to the crash site now."

"Be sure to transport what remains of their cargo. We can always use guns and medicine."

"Sí, Presidente."

Minas ended the call and handed the phone back to his bodyguard.

He sipped the martini with a satisfied smile.

Presently the Lear began to taxi for takeoff.

They'd be home soon, and Minas was bringing good news with him.

Somewhere in Zurich

The man known as Number One, leader of The Trust, stepped out of the black Mercedes and into the crisp Zurich air. He told his driver to wait and carefully shut the door. His old bones seemed to move slower in the cold, but the advancement of age didn't bother him. He took the slowdown as a sign that he should be more careful and complete tasks more deliberately and with forethought. The system seemed to work for him.

He climbed the steps of a stone building overlooking Lake Zurich, with the snow-capped Alps in the far horizon. A wonderful sight to see every day, but this morning Number One did not pause to admire the view. The Trust had a mole somewhere. He needed to find that person and root them out of the organization. The frantic call from Beth Carrington aboard the DC-10 still rang in his ear. The knowledge that the plane had been shot down concerned him greatly.

His keycard opened the large oak doors, and he stepped into a dark hallway with a checkered tile floor and antiques lining the wall. A security guard sat behind a desk. They greeted each other as Number One pressed a button for an elevator and waited.

His real name was Edward Northwood. In a perfect world, his operatives would know him by that name, but to preserve the secrecy of The Trust and his position within, the code name was necessary. His two associates, Numbers Two and Three, carried their numbers for the same reason. His associates were elsewhere today, in separate parts of the world. The three of them had to remain apart in case something happened to one, so the chain of command would not be threatened.

The elevator doors opened, and Northwood stepped inside. The car carried him down two floors into a sub-basement, where the hub of The Trust's intelligence-gathering and operations center was located. He stepped through the open doorway into a room full of wide-screen monitors mounted on the walls, with operators at their own computer workstations, and paused as the whirlwind of voices and activity assaulted his senses. Intelligence wasn't only gathered by humans on location. Computers, satellites, and surveillance cameras did a lot of the work these days. The advances in technology never failed to impress Northwood. He'd had less computing power available to him during the fall of the Berlin Wall than the kids working today.

And they were all kids, men and women in the twenties and thirties, the cream of the crop carefully researched and recruited into The Trust. Some of them had been on the path to join the diplomatic corps or other government agencies such as the CIA. Northwood wanted them before they fell victim to the inevitable government bureaucracy within those organizations and thus became useless.

Had one of them leaked the information about Stiletto

and Carrington's mission by accident or malice?

That was what he had to find out. The small room was all The Trust needed, nothing like the immense and expensive buildings and ops centers used by Western intelligence agencies the world over. The Trust was all about efficiency, but somewhere, they'd made a mistake.

"Good morning, sir."

Northwood nodded at the morning shift supervisor, Melissa Jarrett. She wore a smart blue blazer and skirt combo and had her hair tied back. "We weren't expecting you this morning."

"Exactly," Northwood said. "Let's talk in your office."

She turned and led him to a small office along the wall, with a glass partition looking out on the operations room. She closed the door as Northwood took the seat in front of her cluttered desk.

"You've heard about Stiletto's mission."

"The DC-10. Yes, sir."

"We need to find out how Minas and his goons knew they were coming."

"What are you suggesting?"

"The mission was planned from beginning to end here in the Hub. We need to interview and polygraph everybody involved and find out who they might have spoken to by accident or on purpose."

"You don't think—"

"That's why I included 'accident,' Melissa. Mistakes come from even the most careful people. To keep everybody from getting upset, I suggest the polygraph include the entire staff. Make it look like a routine security scan."

"Of course."

"Meanwhile, we need to try to find out if Stiletto and Carrington survived their crash."

Jarrett nodded. "We'll have to depend on the whisper-stream, sir. We don't have anybody else on the ground there. Maybe we'll hear something in a day or two."

"Let me know as soon as you do," Northwood said, rising from the chair. He grunted and rolled his shoulders back. "It's a terrible thing to get old, Melissa."

"I'm trying to avoid it."

"I failed. I hope you have better luck."

Northwood said good-bye and let himself out of the office. He found the Mercedes and his driver out front where he'd left them and climbed back into the car. He had some thinking to do, so he asked the driver to go in any direction. The driver complied.

Melissa Jarrett stared at the wall ahead of her for a moment. The television on the wall was blank. Normally she had the news on, whichever cable network she picked at random, but not today. News of the assassination attempt and the DC-10 crash had stunned her. She'd not exactly told the truth when she mentioned to Number One that she hadn't expected him. Of course, she had.

She was glad he didn't blame her for losing control

of the ship. She might have only been the morning supervisor, but she took ownership of the Hub more than the other supervisors. Looking out the glass partition, she spotted one of her analysts, Harry Able. She caught his attention and waved him into the office.

"What's happening, chief? Big guy upset?"

Able dropped into the chair vacated by Number One without asking.

Jarrett updated Able on her conversation with "the big guy" and said, "How soon can we start talking to everybody?"

"I'll handle the day crew," Able said, "and I can work with the late crew too if you want to keep this isolated."

"It's better that way, sorry."

"No sweat." He forced a smile. "Not like I have anybody waiting at home, right?"

Jarrett nodded. She could say the same thing about herself. She was older than Harry, though. He still had plenty of time to pick and choose a mate. Her time was running out the closer she crawled, kicking and screaming, to forty.

"Get started," she told him.

"On the double," Able replied.

He left her alone.

Venezuela

Stiletto came to and threw up a little, the mess landing on the front of his shirt. Then he groaned and tried to spit. The taste of scotch, sausage, and cheese filled his mouth, and not in a good way. Everything hurt. He felt around his body, but nothing seemed broken, and he wasn't bleeding. He unstrapped from the chair and crawled to Beth, who was woozy but conscious.

"I smell gas," Beth said.

"Get the door open." Stiletto staggered forward and froze in the cockpit doorway.

The pilot and co-pilot had landed the plane but overshot the clearing and crashed into surrounding trees, one of which had sheared off part of the cockpit and impaled the pilot to his seat. The co-pilot had pieces of glass sticking out of his head and neck.

Stiletto let out a breath. "Sorry, guys."

Beth called his name. She had pushed the door open about two inches before it stopped against a solid object outside. It wouldn't budge, no matter how hard she pushed.

"We can go out through the front."

"The pilots—"

"Didn't make it."

Stiletto collected their packs and a first aid kit from the galley. They had to maneuver around the bodies of the pilot and co-pilot to slide through the gaps at the front of the plane. The nose offered no purchase, and they reached the ground hands-first, then awkwardly rolled away from the plane. Stiletto exited last. He shuffled Beth to a cluster of trees that shaded them from the sun. The ground was dry, and Beth cleared some debris. Smoke from the back of the plane drifted around. Beth coughed. Stiletto and Beth checked their phones. No signal.

"Good news, we lived," Stiletto said. "Bad news, I have no idea where we are."

"Somebody will see the smoke," Beth said.

Stiletto opened the first aid kit. "Let me patch that cut."

Beth scooted toward him.

As soon as Stiletto finished applying the bandage, the center of which immediately sprouted a red spot, they heard a helicopter approaching.

They peered through the trees. The whipping rotor blades grew in volume. The shadow of the chopper passed over them to hover above the wrecked DC-10.

"I don't like this," Beth said.

The Huey helicopter, white in color, bore no forest ranger service or medical markings. The side door opened, and rappelling ropes uncoiled all the way to the ground. Men in black with AK-12 automatic rifles descended on the ropes, four total. Each man disengaged from the ropes and advanced on the Lear with weapons ready.

"Run," Stiletto said, drawing his gun. "Run!"

Beth bolted as Stiletto fired a single round. One of the gunmen dropped, his head splitting open as the Hydra-Shok .45 slug bored through. The remaining three spread out, returning fire, the crackling salvos striking nowhere near Stiletto.

He fired four more random shots and ran after Beth. The automatic weapons continued to crackle sporadically before ceasing. The chopper started flying in Stiletto's direction. Stiletto kept running, breathing hard. Low branches lashed his face.

Beth called his name. He stopped and looked left. She was down behind a fallen tree trunk. Stiletto ran to her, rolling over the top of the trunk. He landed beside her.

"I got one, but there's still three," he said. "Plus the chopper."

"Did you happen to grab one of their weapons?" Beth asked.

"No."

"I lost my pistol in the crash," Beth said. "The only gun we have is yours."

The chopper drifted close, but the canopy of trees kept them covered.

"All right," Stiletto said. "I pity these guys."

The chopper's rotors grew louder.

"Let's get some exercise," Stiletto said.

They pounded across the rough terrain, the ground beginning to slope. Beth stumbled, and Stiletto grabbed her. They ran on. As the incline sharpened, Stiletto dropped beside a tree. The three gunmen were trailing and moving in leap-frog fashion, one going forward while the other two covered. Stiletto sighted and fired, and the three troopers dropped for cover. His shot missed.

Stiletto bolted up the slope.

The chopper flew by off to the right. The tree canopy was thinning. A door gunner leaned out the side.

The odds kept getting better.

Stiletto ran on and caught up with Beth. The ground finally leveled off and they ran briskly, no established trail to make the going easier. Where were they? The ground dipped ahead, and Stiletto directed Beth to it. They dropped low and looked back over the edge.

Beth lay on her back, clutching her side.

"You okay?" Scott said.

"Got a cramp." She winced.

"We'll get tired if we keep running," Stiletto said.

The chopper rotors faded but weren't far away.

"What are you thinking?" Beth asked. A sheen of sweat covered her face and neck, and her shirt stuck to her body.

"There's a door gunner in that helicopter. He'll cut us to shreds," she continued. "Look out!"

Stiletto looked where Beth pointed, and they dropped low. Only the tops of the gunmen's heads were visible, but they were marching closer.

"I want one of those rifles," Beth said. She sank as low as she could. Stiletto kept his eyes forward. One of the troopers exposed too much of his upper body and Stiletto fired. The round hit the man's chest dead-center. The other two opened up, shifting their bursts, the 5.45mm stingers ripping into trees and brush, geysers of dirt sprouting around their position. He fired at the next trooper, but the shot missed. The gunner rolled to better cover. Stiletto dropped to pop the empty magazine out of the Colt and slam home a new one.

Beth crawled out of the dip and moved off to Stiletto's left, staying low as she ran between the trees.

"Dammit, Beth!"

One of the gunmen saw her and swung the AK her way.

"Beth, down!"

The Colt .45 kicked twice. The trooper's head snapped back, painting a nearby tree with specks of red.

A shadow loomed over Stiletto as the chopper roared overhead. The ground exploded as the door gunner swept the ground with heavy machine-gun fire. Beth screamed and covered her face. Chunks of dirt rained down on them. The chopper drifted on, blasting another area about ten yards away.

More shots from the last trooper split the air overhead, the slugs singing like bees. Stiletto put his face into the dirt.

Things kept getting better.

Where was Beth?

Beth Carrington peered through the brush at the dead trooper fifteen yards away. His AK-12, the very latest in the Russian small arms inventory, might as well have been a rare steak, salad on the side and a glass of red wine. Yum.

No sign of the last trooper.

When the chopper's machine gun started hammering, she made her move. The brush snapped and parted as she plowed through. She closed the gap between her and the dead man, diving the last couple of meters. She landed hard and short, crawling the rest of the way.

Then the AK-12 was in her hands.

She popped out the magazine and replaced it with a spare from the man's belt. Staying low, Beth scanned for the last shooter. The crackle of his weapon was ahead and to the right. She advanced, dropping and rolling every few feet, dirt flying each time she hit the ground. A large tree lay ahead. She ran to it and braced against the rough trunk. The last gunner, focused on Stiletto, didn't see her. She stroked the trigger, and the AK-12 bucked against her shoulder.

The burst stitched up the gunner's back to his head, which popped like a crushed watermelon. The man hit the ground. Beth ran over and unbuckled his ammo belt. Blood on the belt smeared her top as she threw it over her shoulder. She snatched the man's AK and ran back to Stiletto.

Now they only faced the chopper.

Stiletto's finger tightened on the trigger, but he lowered the .45 when he saw Beth.

"Merry Christmas," she said, dropping into the dip.

She handed Stiletto a rifle and a couple of magazines.

Stiletto holstered his gun.

The chopper continued its sweep, drifting back and forth.

"We need a clear shot at the pilot," Beth said.

Sunlight beamed through the trees behind them. A clearing. Risky, but worth a try.

"Come on."

Stiletto and Beth ran for the clearing. Stiletto stood in the middle, while Beth took cover near the perimeter. Stiletto raised the AK-12 and fired at the chopper. The chopper turned his way, swinging to the left. The door gunner fired back, strafing the ground beside Stiletto. He stayed on his feet. His next burst bounced around the edges of the doorway. The chopper continued its turn. Beth fired at the back of the engine, and the shots landed on target. Sparks flashed. Smoke billowed out.

The chopper turned again. Stiletto fired at the Plexiglas bubble in front. The chopper swung wide, the engine straining. Stiletto ran to Beth, tackling her and covering her body with his as the chopper fell through the trees. The rotors whined as they slammed into the trunks, and the body of the chopper exploded when it struck the earth.

The heat of the blast and pieces of flaming debris washed over them. The ground shook.

When the shockwave passed, Stiletto and Beth scrambled up. They smiled at each other.

"You're pretty good in a fight," Beth said.

"Not so bad yourself. Thanks for the rifle."

She smiled.

"I suppose now we have to go find some rebels," he said, "and see if they can spare some men and trucks to come collect what's left of the supplies."

She knelt down to grab a map from her pack. Spreading it out on the ground, they performed basic land navigation to approximate their position.

"Bad news," she said, "is that we're very far from where we intended to land."

"Is there good news?"

"Yes." She studied the map another moment, then folded the paper, stowed it, and slung her pack. "Follow me. It will be a long march, but there's a farm not far from here the rebels often use. They'll have radio equipment."

"Let's go."

They started walking.

CHAPTER FIVE

The breeze hadn't yet carried away the smells of breakfast. The rustling trees suggested tranquility, but there was no such thing in the camp. What there was instead was cold anger.

Colonel Ciro Verduzco wandered along the rows of tents. He was dressed in green camo with a matching hat tilted forward on his head, his combat boots muddy, and his face streaked with more worry lines than sweat. They were small tents, holding three men each, although some of the women fighters had their own area as well. The troops were mostly outside, fixing gear, cleaning weapons, talking, smoking, and giving him the evil eye when they thought he wasn't looking. But he saw them. Each stare felt like a barbed whip against his back.

The forest camp was yet another in a long line of similar camps Verduzco's forces had set up throughout the area, deep in the woods, the terrain fierce, rugged, and hostile. The ground beneath Verduzco's feet was hard-packed, insects never far from them. The bigger four-legged animals were a different matter entirely, but they at least stayed away during daylight hours.

And the heat of the sun, mercifully, was subdued by the solid canopy of trees overhead.

Verduzco served as the overall leader of the rebel army locked in a battle with the forces of Lazaro Minas, fighting for the freedom of their little country.

But Verduzco had paused hostilities on the part of the rebels for over a month. All they'd done was run from one camp to another, trying to stay a step ahead of the death squads.

The troops blamed Verduzco. They were tiring of his excuses, but he had no choice.

And it was his fault, too. There was no way he wanted to argue the point. He was keeping secrets from his fighters, and the weight of leadership of such a ragtag crew was made worse by what he kept hidden from them.

The war had started three years ago after what Venezuelans referred to as the "April Massacre."

The rebellion officially began as a march and protest in the capital city, where citizens spoke out about the increasingly depressed economy and their suffering under the stagnation while the politicians and other higher-ups seemed to have plenty of what the citizens lacked.

The protest turned into three days of destructive rioting, and then the tanks had rolled into the city.

The soldiers had direct orders from Minas: Stop the rioters.

That was when the shooting started.

Verduzco had, at one time, kept the number of dead in his head as a reminder about what they were fighting against. But after so many years, and so many more dead, the number was lost to him.

The rebels assembled quietly once the smoke had cleared. It was easy to organize groups of people willing to fight. It was not easy to acquire weapons. The government learned of the rebellion when the first batches of arms smuggled into the region were intercepted by Minas' police forces. But the fighters persisted. Their first strikes against government strongholds had produced mixed results in terms of solid victories, but had communicated clearly that the people were going to fight back and Minas' days were numbered.

Three years later, Verduzco wasn't as boastful as he'd been in the early days.

He'd steadily risen through the ranks, in part because other leaders kept getting killed, and now led the entire rebel army. And he had a certain vulnerability that Minas had recently exploited. That was why his men eyed him with disdain as he walked along the tent row. His grip on the troops was slipping. It might be better, he thought, to step aside and let somebody else run the war from now on. Perhaps his fighting days were over.

The troops looked good otherwise. Fit. Fed. Eager. He wished the whole of Venezuela supported their effort, but the majority did not. The majority wanted the government handouts. The majority were willing to cede their God-given freedom to people like Minas in exchange for comfort and shelter, but there was neither in Venezuela, not after Hurricane Margaret. The underground minority the rebels depended on for supplies and information supported the fight, but there weren't enough of them.

Verduzco reached the end of the tent row and stopped face-to-face with his second-in-command, Major Gustavo Arencibia.

"The troops look good," Verduzco said.

"They are not happy, Colonel."

"I know."

"Either we break your son out of prison, or you have to make a sacrifice, sir. Look around you. They're ready to fight anything you point at."

"Maybe even me?"

Arencibia stuttered as he tried to reply. "Of course not. But a change of command—"

"May be necessary," Verduzco said. "Let Minas exploit your weaknesses for a change."

Verduzco's weakness was his adult son, who had commanded his own rebel cell, holding the rank of captain. Minas' forces had recently captured Carlos, and they were holding him on The Island, the prison of sitting off the coast of Venezuela. There were a lot of rebel prisoners on the island. The capture was not a secret. Arencibia and the other rebel commanders were well aware Carlos had been taken. The secret Verduzco kept to himself, however, was not known. Minas had communicated quietly that Carlos would not be harmed if Verduzco ceased hostilities. Verduzco knew the request was not made because Minas wanted to stop the war. That wasn't his reason at all. He'd gladly keep the war going because it provided terrific opportunities for propaganda and turning the public against the fighting.

No. Minas needed the fighting to cool off while he begged the United Nations for money.

Money that would never be used to help the citizens of Venezuela, but would instead line the pockets of Minas and his cronies.

"If you need to step down, Colonel—"

"Not now, Major."

"If we stop fighting, Minas wins. Do you want that?"

Verduzco said nothing.

"Is that what you want, Colonel?"

Verduzco didn't know what to say.

For three years, he'd sent his fighters into battle. Some had survived. Some had not. Carlos knew the risks, same as everybody else.

But now that his own flesh-and-blood was in the hands of the enemy, Verduzco felt paralyzed.

He had already lost his wife. She'd died during the April Massacre. Died in his arms, riddled with bullets from a soldier's gun.

From that day forward, Verduzco had sworn he'd see the end of Minas, no matter what. The thought that he might lose his only son caused pain deep down where Verduzco didn't think it was possible to hurt.

He couldn't keep the major or anybody else at bay for much longer. His time was running out.

Major Gustavo Arencibia understood what his colonel was going through. Everybody in the rebel movement had family in danger, but nobody else wanted to stop fighting because of that. In fact, they wanted to fight more to end the danger.

He simply did not understand why the colonel was having such a hard time.

But there were other matters that required attention, such as a missing airplane full of guns and medicine that, if the rebels didn't locate it, might spell the end of the fighting altogether, never mind the colonel's personal problems.

"There is something else we should talk about."

Verduzco looked relieved. "Yes?"

"The plane with the medicine and guns."

"Has it landed?"

"It's been shot down."

Verduzco closed his eyes. "Oh, no."

"Should we send a search party to look for survivors? See if anything is left of the cargo?"

Verduzco opened his eyes. "Weren't they supposed to contact you when they landed?"

"Yes, Colonel."

"If they survived, don't you think they'd have done so?"

"Depends on their level of injury. We can't let that plane or cargo fall into Minas' hands."

Verduzco nodded. "Do we know where the plane crashed?"

"Our sources in the palace gave us an approximate area."

"If the palace knows about the plane, did they also send a search party?"

"Probably. Our sources didn't know."

"Ask for volunteers. Tell them to expect an engagement."

The major nodded and called the forces to line up in front of him. He glanced at Colonel Verduzco, only to see the colonel take the opportunity to move out of sight.

The heat felt good. An honest tropical heat with enough humidity to make the shirt stick to your back.

Lazaro Minas loved the heat.

He and his entourage stepped off the private jet at Simón Bolívar International Airport. Tanks surrounded the property, and armed soldiers were everywhere. The airport was a prime rebel target. The show of force had, so far, kept them from attacking.

After a short walk across the tarmac to a line of armored SUVs, Minas started to loosen his tie. He had a meeting with his ministers within the hour. He checked his watch. They should have arrived at the hacienda already. He wouldn't tolerate stragglers.

The presidential convoy traveled along a dirt road leaving the back side of the airport, then made a right turn onto a paved road heading north toward the presidential palace. The trip was delayed as they navigated around obstructions left over from Hurricane Margaret that had not yet been cleared, and Minas made a note of the location to pass along to the interior minister.

People walking along either side of the road waved at the motorcade, Minas smiling and waving back despite the window tint. It made him feel better. Not all of the country stood against him, only a violent group of pirates who thought they could run the nation better than him. He didn't think the rebel leaders were truly any different than he was. They had their own agenda, and if they ever took power, the promises made to their supporters would ring as hollow as his own. But people sure kept listening when you told them what they wanted to hear.

It was a trick he had learned early in his career with the National Assembly. The citizens were quite simple, unable to govern themselves because their minds didn't grasp the responsibility involved. Better to encourage them to rest and relax, let somebody else do the heavy lifting and take on the responsibilities. In return, the government provided jobs, food, goods, and medical care, and the people accepted the arrangement despite their inability to admit they were powerless. Minas often joked that if people were truly allowed to control their own destinies, society would quickly deteriorate into tribes and war. In his own way, Minas saw himself as protecting his society. If that meant performing certain dirty tricks or acts of violence against those who opposed him, such as sending them to work camps or shooting the worst of the lot, he only did so because it was best for the people.

Happy people, happy country, happy Presidente.

That happiness required constant vigilance. Recently, Minas' security agents had discovered a group of university students using a smartphone smuggled into the country to document police beatings and even the work of one of his death squads as they raided a suspected rebel home. The students had planned to upload the footage to a website and let the world see what was really happening prior to Minas' speech at the United Nations. Luckily, the students were captured, the phone destroyed, and order restored once the students had been shipped to a work camp. Minas had a feeling the CIA was responsible and had provided the smartphone. He had no proof, but who needed proof when the CIA was already in the country and actively working against him?

But he was having the last laugh now that the Americans had voted with the UN to send money.

Fools.

They'd done it to avoid embarrassing questions, however. He understood. Saving face. If they objected too harshly, maybe somebody would discover they were violating international law by attempting to overthrow his "legally-elected" government.

The convoy presently turned up a long driveway, well-manicured lawn on either side, the hacienda ahead surrounded by open country and a stunning view of a mountain range in the distance, as well as Caracas. The convoy stopped in the center courtyard of the hacienda, polished marble stones making up the floor, with a fountain in the center.

Minas had designed the home so that his bedroom, at the tip of the V, faced the mountains, with a pool directly below his balcony.

Minas and his entourage exited the vehicles, and he climbed a set of stairs to the second floor, advancing down the outside walkway to his bedroom, passing three soldiers stationed along the way. He stopped to greet each one. Treat the troops well, and they'll die for you. Minas took a few minutes to splash some water on his face and change clothes, trading the formal suit for a less formal button-down shirt and khaki trouser option. He left the shirt untucked.

A knock at the bedroom door. Two taps, pause, a third. One of the troopers. Minas opened the door.

"General Florez to see you, sir."

Minas nodded and stepped back to allow his number two, General Vitorio Florez, to step into the bedroom. As usual, the general wore his full-dress uniform, his chest decorated with medals, his boots brightly polished, not a hair on his head out of place.

"Welcome home, Presidente," Florez said.

"The new trees look good."

"Thank you, Presidente."

"I'd like the fountain working by the end of the week."

"It will be functional by noon tomorrow, Presidente."

"Are the ministers waiting for me?"

"Present and accounted for. Nobody arrived late."

"Very good. Why are you here, General?"

"I must report bad news."

Minas raised an eyebrow.

Florez explained that the crew sent to recover the survivors of the CIA plane crash were dead, and the survivors, if there were any, had vacated the area. A follow-up crew only found the bodies of the pilots, still in the cockpit of the plane.

"Is your team still in the area of the crash?"

"Yes, Presidente. If the CIA people went off to meet their rebel contacts, they will return to the plane."

"And your team will be waiting for them."

"Yes. Yes, indeed."

"Well done, General. No survivors. Anything else?"

"That is all. I wanted you to know before the meeting with the ministers."

"And I appreciate it." Minas held the door open. "We'll talk again after the meeting, I'm sure."

"Your wife—"

Minas frowned. "What about her?"

"She asked me to tell you to see her after the meeting."

"After?"

"She did say before, sir, but—"

"Of course, she did." Minas smiled. Florez half-smiled. Florez left the room, and Minas closed the door behind him.

Minas sighed and turned to look at himself in a full-length mirror on the wall behind him. He loved Clarissa, his wife, the blonde American fireball, but she either she didn't understand that not even she ordered El Presidente to do anything he didn't want to, or she was flaunting the fact that she understood the pecking order south of the border but didn't care.

He should have her beaten. Or beat her himself. Whatever it took for her to learn her place.

But not even Minas could order that. In a lot of ways, she was his one weakness. He'd calmly tell her that the people's business had to come first, but they had all the time left over. She'd understand, or not. If not, he'd tell her again sometime.

Minas smoothed the front of his shirt and left the bedroom.

Time to share the good news with the ministers. Crossing the bedroom to a wall with a connecting door, he stepped through into the conference room.

CHAPTER SIX

The conference room only had three walls.

The fourth wall had been removed, revealing part of the mountain view and allowing cooling air to filter inside. And insects. Burning candles on the table repelled at least the worst of them, but now and then, one that seemed immune to the fumes flew around and harassed those around the table.

Large framed pictures on the walls showed major events in the administration of Lazaro Minas, featuring him speaking before crowds, dedicating government buildings, and mixing with the people. He refrained from hanging large portraits of himself anywhere in the Presidential Palace. Even his ego didn't go that far, but he did insist on those portraits within other government buildings, and in public where the people tended to gather most.

Minas strode proudly into the room, his arms wide open and a big smile on his face. The men seated around the table broke into applause and rose to greet him. Hand-shakes and hugs followed. Minas accepted the attention with gladness. He was a conquering hero and deserved the adulation. The government ministers would be even more excited once he told them the news. They settled back into their seats, while Minas assumed his standing position at the head of the table, the open wall—and na-ture—behind him.

"The trip could not have been more successful," Minas began. He watched the faces of the government ministers. Interior, Defense, Communications, Education—they were all there. Men he'd known for decades, served with for decades. They knew most of each other's secrets, good and bad. Minas didn't think any of them would ever betray him, but he still had them spied on regularly to make sure they weren't cheating him or plotting against him. "We will have the money we ask for, but it comes with a caveat. UN observers will be here to make sure the money and relief supplies reach the people they are supposed to reach."

Murmurs of agreement. "There was no other way," Minas said. "It's standard protocol, and to protest might have jeopardized the outcome. Now," he pointed at Gar-cia, Minister of the Interior, "your department will have to work to keep the streets clear and the airport ready to receive aircraft. The runways need to be free of debris at all times, and our air traffic controllers fresh and alert."

Garcia gave one curt nod.

To the Defense Minister, Octavio, Minas said, "Rebel activity. What's it been like since I was gone?"

"Very little. Our forces have been scouring the countryside looking for camps. We've made one or two raids, trying to drive them deeper into the forest. I think having the son of the rebel leader locked up is helping."

"As I thought," Minas said. "Good. It needs to stay that way while the UN is here. We need a strong presence in the streets, and keep them on the run. The UN will not be wandering into the forests, so do whatever you need to do away from prying eyes."

Octavio nodded.

"Other business?"

Each minister had a folder on the table before him, and Garcia, the Minister of the Interior, opened his.

"Go ahead, Minister Garcia," Minas directed.

Garcia put a set of bifocals on the edge of his nose and began reading from notes. Minas paced back and forth while he spoke.

"Our survey crews have discovered a large vein of copper in the northern part of the country," he said.

"How much?"

"We can't be sure without going underground, and we lack the needed equipment."

Minas stopped pacing and sighed. It was the same old story. Venezuela had resources to spare. What it didn't have was the necessary equipment and infrastructure to take advantage of those resources. What little mining activity actually taking place was nearly costing more than it returned. The Russians had tried to help but grew frustrated with Minas for not parting with as much of the take as they wanted.

"Perhaps we can make a deal with the Chinese?" Garcia offered.

The table murmured. Some supported the suggestion, but others shook their heads.

"They'll want too much, just like the Russians," Minas said.

Chatter back and forth, suggestions fired off. Minas kept shaking his head. Finally, he said, "If the deposit is that good, is, in fact, as good as the recent gold deposit we also found, then we need to keep as much as we can for ourselves. And for Venezuela," he added to quiet laughter. "Do we have an estimate on how much new mining equipment will cost us?"

Garcia quoted a number that stunned even Minas.

"We have nowhere near that to begin with," El Presidente said.

The Minister of Communications suggested, "We can divert some of the UN money."

Minas laughed. "All the money is going to be diverted, my friend, but how much of a loss are we willing to take?"

"The options, as I see them," said Garcia, "are to put forth whatever effort we can, or allow other countries to help us in exchange for mining rights."

"That's unacceptable."

"Do you have a suggestion, Presidente?"

"There are other people we can turn to for liquid cash, and they won't take as much in return as Russia or China," Minas said. "Some of them will be attending my wife's birthday party to talk about other arrangements I have in mind. I think I will add this to our conversations."

Garcia blinked.

"Is there a problem?"

"Can these people be trusted?" asked the Minister of the Interior. "We're taking their hard currency to provide sanctuary. How do we know they won't somehow betray us?"

"The kind of people we're talking about will know better than to kick us in our faces," Minas said, "especially since we're on such good terms with the rest of the world right now. If we suddenly announce the presence of wanted fugitives in our country, we may lose hard money in the short term, but the long-term goodwill we'll earn will make up for it. They won't have any choice."

"Unless they say no."

"Then we must make every effort," Minas said, "to make sure they don't say no. I'm not leaving millions and millions of dollars in oil, copper, and gold in the mud. Besides, what man in his right mind will say no to a guaranteed return on investment?"

On that, everybody agreed.

Minas' wife was always a sight to behold.

They were exactly the same age, but she seemed younger, probably because of the lack of stress leadership caused. Minas' face had worry lines; Clarissa's did not. The only thing she worried about was making sure she was never seen in public wearing the same outfit twice.

She wore a long white dress belted at the waist with gold braid. Her legs and shoulders bare, the dress unable to hide her wonderful curves. Long, curly blonde hair cascaded down her back, offset by fiery green eyes. The people loved her. She often went to the streets, with her security entourage quite discreet, to mix and mingle with Venezuela's citizens and further the cause of her husband and his policies. Making an effort to read to school children and help with hurricane recovery only made them love her more. If Minas was having difficulty with a policy proposal or with the rebels, he sent Clarissa out to smooth the ruffled feathers. She never failed to do so.

But she had to work hard, he knew, to put up that public façade. She was very stubborn and otherwise self-centered. Mixing with "those people" wasn't something she enjoyed.

"Hello, husband," she said from the window-side lounger in the large living room. The drapes were all open. Sunlight streamed through, the crystal-clear window glass allowing another spectacular view of the countryside.

She did not rise. She held a glass of red wine and was swishing the liquid in impatient circles like a cat communicating displeasure by how it flicked its tail.

"Don't I get a kiss?" Minas asked, approaching slowly. He stopped midway. The mountain did not go to Mohammed.

"I'm sure you got plenty of hugs and kisses from the ministers," she said. "Didn't you get my message?"

"Yes," he said. He crossed to a small bar and poured his own drink from a bottle of Johnny Walker Red. He turned back to her. She stared at him.

Her last name had been Gunderson when he'd met her in Hollywood during a trip to Los Angeles to convince film studios that Venezuela would make a great filming location, with assorted tax breaks and protections to sweeten the deal, long before the trouble with the rebels had broken out.

Hollywood had passed, but that was how he had met Clarissa. She was a secretary to one of the studio bigwigs who'd turned Minas down. Minas always chuckled, thinking he'd stolen the man's Girl Friday instead.

He provided her a wonderful life in Venezuela, but she was never satisfied.

"We need to talk about my birthday party," she said.

"I told you to plan it however you wanted."

"What I don't want," she said, "are your hooligans attending."

Minas blinked. "My what?"

"The crooks and smugglers and whoever else from Evil Villain Casting, Incorporated that you're bringing in."

"We have business to discuss."

"Not on my birthday, Lazaro!"

He sipped his drink.

"Will you come and sit down already?"

He took the couch across from her, a glass coffee table dividing them.

With a huff, she left her lounger and dropped beside him, careful not to spill her wine.

"Damn you," she exclaimed.

"If Venezuela is going to recover from the hurricane, we need investment. The people I am inviting will be offered a chance to invest in our infrastructure in return for a share of our mining profits," he said.

"You're giving them a place to hide and charging a lot of money for the privilege. This has nothing to do with mining profits."

"It's a bonus." He winked.

"They'll bring trouble, Lazaro. We already have enough trouble with the rebels."

"They've been quiet since we captured the leader's son."

"That won't last forever!"

"It will last long enough for our forces to make them hurt so bad they'll give up fighting."

"You're a lousy liar."

He looked at her sharply. "What do you mean?"

"There are rumors, honey. Rumors you promised a ceasefire in exchange for not harming Verduzco's kid."

A hot flush crawled up Minas' neck.

"Who is saying this?"

"Everybody. And nobody." She made a dismissive wave and sipped her wine. "Just what I heard," she added.

He stared at her. Her hand shook as she sipped more wine, almost gulping down what remained. He'd never raised a hand to her. A look of rebuke was always enough to put her off-balance and make her realize her errors.

"I will find out the source of this rumor, my dear, and deal with him—or her—harshly."

"It's not me."

"Who is it?"

"I told you, it's just what I heard."

Minas set down his glass and fumed. Rumors were normal, but they were usually a minor annoyance and could be disproven with time or action. He had no intention of letting the rebels rest and regroup while he played some sort of head game with Verduzco; it wasn't productive. He'd ordered that the rebels be pushed back far into the countryside, away from the prying eyes of the UN. If his ministers were the source or had heard the same thing as Clarissa, the action of those orders would certainly calm the chatter.

But part of what made his wife's statement so difficult was that what she'd heard was true.

The war was, frankly, intoxicating. Having a constant enemy to fight made him look good with every victory. The fighting gave him something to make speeches about while trying to convince the population not supporting the rebels that they should remain loyal and report rebel activity. The rebels were criminals who deserved to be hanged, and they had no interest in Venezuela's future, only their own enrichment at the expense of the people.

The irony of the words was never lost on Minas and always gave him a good laugh.

Without a war, without rebels to blame the country's troubles on, Minas might lose a reliable power play.

Capturing the Verduzco son, Carlos, had been a stroke of luck and nothing more. The man had been rounded up with other rebels in the city, unidentified at the time, but recognized soon after. He'd had his troops post photographs of the captured man in the forest along known rebel routes so word might get back to Verduzco. Then Minas had asked for a private chat with one of the captured fighters, anyone but Carlos, and put a coded message in the man's hand. That particular rebel had been released and allowed to return, unfollowed, to whichever camp he found. Verduzco would have no trouble decoding the message, which said he had no intention of harming his son as long as the fighting ceased. Minas needed the ceasefire to convince the UN to help Venezuela.

Obviously, the message had been read by more eyes than Verduzco's, and word had quietly spread, like a virus. He hadn't said a word about the decision to Clarissa, yet she somehow knew. Minas had to prove the rumor false by action. To let on that he knew about the chatter would only make the rumor grow.

But how had it spread so quickly? Who else was talking? Was it somebody close to him, trying to undermine his leadership?

Minas took a long drink.

Clarissa said, "Whatever you want to do for my party is fine."

"I never said it was negotiable, dear."

Clarissa cursed.

Minas finished his drink and set the glass down again.

"You haven't asked me how my trip went. Or did somebody already tell you?"

She shrank against the couch pillows. "How was your trip, Lazaro?"

He provided a truncated update, promising that the relief supplies probably wouldn't arrive until well after her party. Even the UN had a crap-ton of red tape to go through in order to send a relief mission, and the nations that pledged money had to put the funds together. The first planes might not arrive for two or three months.

"You did well, Lazaro."

He smiled. Faint praise was still praise.

"It's been a long day, and I am tired," he said. "Leading a country is very hard."

She leaned forward, almost too quickly, put her unfinished wine on the table, and leaned close to him. Her right hand reached for his crotch.

"Care to tell me what else is hard?"

Typical. But Minas didn't refuse.

They smelled death before reaching the farm.

Beth Carrington hadn't exaggerated. The march was long. Stiletto's legs were aching by the time the ground finally flattened, and then they found a crude dirt road that Beth said they should follow. The deep ruts on either side showed more evidence of carriage wheels than motor vehicle tires. The path hadn't entirely been cleared of foliage, but the movement of the carriages had tamped it down enough that Stiletto and Beth could walk without anything snapping at their ankles. The rest of the forest surrounded them, the afternoon brightness helping visibility in all directions. Stiletto didn't want to be making this trek in the middle of the night, when shadows often took the form of two-legged predators with guns who knew the land better than he. The captured Kalashnikov rifles brought some comfort, but not enough. They had to watch out for gunmen, traps, and trip wires linked to explosives that might cut their mission short.

And then the stench hit them.

"Oh, no," Beth said.

Stiletto grit his teeth. "Come on," he said, picking up the pace. Beth trotted to keep up.

Scott stopped short at the edge of the dirt road where it met a clearing—the front yard of the farm, all dirt. A house sat ahead of them, and to the left, a barn. Near the barn was a pen with four cows, and flies buzzed over the cows. The cattle had been slaughtered by heavy-caliber bullets, and lay on their sides, the ground below them a mix of brown and red.

The bodies lay in the yard.

Four bodies in total. Flies buzzed around them, too.

The house had also taken a series of bullet strikes. Holes blown in the walls, the windows shot out.

Beth covered her mouth and nose.

Stiletto took in the carnage and absently lowered his weapon. Then he snapped the AK to his shoulder and grabbed Beth, pulling her down beside him.

"What do you see?" she said.

"Nothing yet. This only happened a day or two ago, and the death squad might be waiting to see who else might show up."

"Did you hear that?"

"What?"

"Somebody—a noise."

She bolted forward. Stiletto didn't call after her or follow. He started moving around the perimeter, carefully checking every bush and tree trunk for any sign of further threats. He found plenty of boot prints and spent shell casings, mostly around the four bodies. The death squad had opened fire from two or three points, hosing the four people, and the ground was saturated with what must have been ninety percent of their blood. Two men, one older, one younger; two women, one older, one very young. No sign of the victims' weapons, if they'd had any. No sign of a battle, either. Why the death squad hadn't torched the buildings, Stiletto didn't know. They possibly didn't want a forest fire raging for days on end. There was no evidence that any death squad troops had fallen and been dragged away. The family had been executed. This was the enemy he was fighting, one who would slaughter an unarmed family simply because they gave aid and comfort to rebel forces.

Somebody running. Stiletto pressed his back to the wall of the house and held the AK at the ready, but relaxed when he saw Beth turn the corner. She didn't have her rifle.

"I found it!" she said.

"What?"

"That noise I heard was the radio! In the barn, come on."

This time, Stiletto followed behind her, his eyes never looking in one direction for too long as she led him into the barn. Bales and bales of hay inside, an aisle down the center. Beth stopped in the middle of the floor at an open trap door. "Watch your step," she said.

He went down the steps into a cramped room, the dirt walls braced with steel cable. She sat on a metal folding chair in front of a short-wave radio, and Stiletto finally saw her rifle propped up against the table supporting the radio set. Lights glowed behind the short-wave dials, the illumination barely filling the hole. The only light really came from above, and there was enough dust floating around to make Stiletto's nose and eyes itch.

This radio made them a target. Stiletto clenched his jaw a little tighter.

Minas could present himself to the rest of the world as pure as the snow in a Minnesota winter, but Stiletto would see him turn red and expose his dark heart for all to see.

The radio speaker hummed. Beth adjusted a small microphone so it was about a finger-length away from her mouth. Stiletto figured she'd memorized the contact procedure long before they'd departed Miami. She pressed a button and started talking.

"Firefly to Spider's Web."

She let up on the button. No static, but nothing else encouraging, either. There was only silence.

She tried again.

"Firefly to Spider's Web at location A223, can you still hear me?"

Stiletto went halfway up the steps to scan the interior of the barn, the barrel of the AK-12 moving with his gaze.

"We have you, Firefly. This is Spider's Web."

Beth told the other person where they were, and that there were no survivors. She added, "We need help getting back to the plane. We still have supplies to unload."

"We have a team heading for you," said Spider's Web. "I'll redirect them to your location. Keep your eyes open. We have word the enemy is heading for the crash site as well."

Stiletto raised an eyebrow when the last line caught

his attention. Good. A chance to give back some of what these animals have been dishing out.

"Who should I ask for when the team arrives?" Beth said.

"Sergeant Castillo is in charge."

"We'll be standing by, Spider. Firefly over and out."

Beth cut off the radio set and left the chair without grabbing her rifle. Stiletto reminded her. She grabbed the AK and followed him back to the surface.

"Let's find a shovel," Stiletto said.

"For what?"

"While we're waiting, I'm going to bury those bodies."

CHAPTER SEVEN

Only the mix of blood and mud in the yard marked where the bodies had fallen.

Scott had dug four graves in an area behind the house next to a vegetable garden, his shirt now drenched with sweat and stained red as he and Beth sat on the porch. They'd found bottled water inside the house, and sipped it while sitting in an exhausted daze. Beth had helped carry the bodies around back and drop them into the ground. He felt awful for that part, but there was no other way to get them back there. Lastly, Stiletto had filled the holes and marked the spots with rocks he found in the garden.

"Do you know who those people were?" he said. His energy was gone. The bench under the awning in front of the house shielded them from the sun, but it was still hot.

"No," she said. "This was an emergency contact point. We'd have identified ourselves with a passcode."

Stiletto nodded. Maybe somebody else will know their names. They need more than rocks for markers.

He swallowed another mouthful of warm water. He wanted to drink faster, but after all his effort, he needed to take it slow. His Combat Government pistol rested on his right leg. The AK-12 leaned against the wall to his left, his backpack with his spare ammo, cigars, clean clothes and other supplies next to the rifle. If the enemy showed up again, he wasn't sure he'd have the strength to lift either of the weapons. He'd worked hard digging the graves. Maybe too hard. He'd taken no breaks. The victims deserved better than to lay under the sun, the indignity of their executions on display. Stiletto didn't think he deserved a break. Not until they were taken care of.

Scott would have no such mercy for Minas.

Or any of his soldiers.

None at all.

"Your contact," Stiletto said, "mentioned enemy troops heading for the crash site. Did they stop here first, looking for us?"

"Probably." Beth stared ahead at nothing. She was as disheveled as he, but had taken time to brush off and straighten her clothes, whereas Scott hadn't.

Stiletto let out a breath. Flies buzzed all around, but especially in the center of the yard and over the dead cows.

The stench hadn't faded either, lingering in the still air, magnified by the heat. That would go away only when Stiletto finally had Lazaro Minas in front of a gun.

Somebody marched up the road. Somebody alone. He wasn't being quiet. His boots crunched on the dirt.

Stiletto grabbed his pistol and left the seat, dropping to one knee behind the porch railing, his arms resting on top. His tight grip tensed the muscles in his arm, and he felt them starting to shake under the strain. His legs ached too, but the sights of the Colt Combat Government zeroed on a lone soldier in camouflage who stepped onto the property. Scott wouldn't go down without taking as many of the enemy with him as he could.

The soldier looked young, but the green-and-black camo paint on his face concealed his features. An automatic rifle was slung around his shoulder, and his left arm was raised.

"Flash!" he called. "Flash!"

Beth shouted back, "Thunder!"

Stiletto relaxed, taking a moment to catch his breath before using the rail to boost himself up. He holstered the pistol and turned to grab the AK and his pack. Beth was already running to the solider. Stiletto trotted after her to keep up. She doesn't waste a second.

"Sergeant Castillo?"

"Señorita Carrington?"

"That's me," Beth said. "This is my associate, Scott Stiletto."

Stiletto and Castillo shook hands. The soldier's hands felt sweaty. Castillo then let out a shrill whistle. Foliage rustled around them and more camouflaged soldiers rose to full height, weapons at the ready. They carried a mix of American M-16A1 rifles that had to be over twenty years old, newer M-4s, and older Russian Kalashnikovs. Castillo's rifle was an antique, a bolt-action Mosin-Nagant 91/30 dating back to the First World War, but Stiletto didn't doubt the man knew how to make the most of the devastating weapon. The potent 7.62x54R cartridge launched by the 24-inch barrel had more power than the dinky rounds in any of the other weapons carried by his men.

"You are a good man with a pistol, I can tell," Castillo told Stiletto. "But we had you covered long before I got here."

Stiletto let out a laugh. "I'd have deserved it if you shot me, Sergeant."

"Where are Hector and his family?"

"We buried them around back," Stiletto said. "I'm glad you know their names. I marked the graves with stones."

"We will take a moment and properly label those stones," Castillo said. "I did not know them personally, but they have aided our struggle since the beginning. They will be remembered with honor when the war is over."

"Follow me," Scott said. He showed Castillo, who produced a black Sharpie marker from the hip pouch he wore cross-body, where the graves were, and explained how he'd buried the family. Older man, young man; older woman, young girl. Castillo knelt beside each crude square of fresh dirt and wrote their names on the stone.

When he finished, he and Stiletto stood quietly for a moment.

There is always a war somewhere. Wars everywhere produced victims like the ones in the ground before him. He could fight lawlessness and tyranny in whatever form he found it, using whatever tools were most quickly available, but like an avalanche, he had nothing to truly halt the damage The Enemy in all its forms inflicted. Sometimes he only collected the pieces they left behind, as in this case. He didn't know the family, didn't understand their full contribution to the rebel cause, but he hurt for them. He hurt because they'd been killed by a death squad searching for him and Beth. He hurt because one man stopping an avalanche was impossible, but he had to try anyway.

As he and the soldier stood in reflection, Stiletto knew the list of victims wasn't going to grow much longer. Because he was there now. He had tools at his disposal and an enemy in his sights, and by the time he left Venezuela, only the good would remain to take back their land and create their own destinies.

A tough goal, yeah. The enemy had its own tools, and viciousness to spare.

Up close, despite the camo paint on his face, Castillo looked young—in his early twenties, by Scott's guess. There were better things for a twenty-year-old to do than fight a war, but Stiletto recognized a resolve in the soldier that was stronger than steel. He could be doing anything else; he might have even gone to the United States or elsewhere, seeking his fortune. Instead, he stayed home to fight, because Venezuela was home, the hell with other countries, and you can't turn your back on your own people. Stiletto expected the same in the other rebels he had yet to meet, and especially their leader.

And resolve defeated viciousness any day of the week.

Castillo said, "We have to go."

Stiletto agreed.

Thankfully, Castillo and his crew had arrived in trucks, two of them. Most of the soldiers fit on the first truck. The second, the sergeant explained, was to carry back supplies and weapons from the crashed DC-10.

"I hope there will be enough," Castillo said as they drove. "We need medicine badly. The guns we can live without for a little while longer."

Sitting in the open back of the Ma Deuce was like sliding into a comfortable bed for Stiletto, though Beth's grimace showed she wasn't having as good a time since the raised exhaust ports beside the cabin belched black smoke into the air. The scent of the exhaust wasn't pleasing, but it beat the stink of death back at the farm.

The trucks moved slowly through the forest, navigating the dirt roads, complete with various obstacles such as fallen tree trunks. Scouts ahead on foot cleared the path, making sure there were no bomb traps. The trucks sometimes stopped for ten or more minutes while the scouts removed such traps. The tree trunks required everybody's attention to cut and move, although Castillo did put three men on security detail. They were young, like him, one maybe sixteen. His body wasn't big enough for his uniform. It was a sad sight, yet an inspiring one.

The truck bed rocked them back and forth. They all sat close to one another, ten troops in total plus Stiletto and Beth. The deuce in front was empty to make room for the recovered supplies and weapons. Each belch of the exhaust pipes sent a wave of heat flying over them, making a hot day even worse.

"Minas' soldiers are fierce," Castillo said. "There are tripwires everywhere."

"We've been fortunate, then," Stiletto said, and he talked briefly about their march from the crash site to the farm.

Castillo chuckled quietly. "You must be here for a reason, Señor Stiletto."

Scott made no comment. He was here for his usual reasons, sure, but the sergeant made it sound like something else was in play. Something almost spiritual, perhaps, that had brought Scott to this fight. Scott wasn't sure what to think about that. He certainly believed in the guiding hand of the Almighty and had been through too many scrapes not to think there was something or somebody watching out for him, but in all honesty, he was too nervous to confront the theory directly. Such pondering forced a man to ask questions about himself, and Stiletto was afraid of the answers. It was easier to fight somebody else's battle than deal with his own.

"You okay?" Beth asked.

She sat across from him on the wooden bench on the other side of the truck.

"Tired," Stiletto said.

Castillo grunted. "Aren't we all?" he said.

The hair on the back of Stiletto's neck stood up.

The wreckage of the DC-10 lay about thirty yards ahead, deep in the forest. But there were threats in the area, too, and close. Very close.

Stiletto lay on his stomach, hidden in the brush, a mix of grass tips and rocks digging into his skin. Castillo and his soldiers had spread out widely. They had arrived over an hour ago, leaving the trucks farther back and marching into the area, then taking cover and waiting. Beth and the truck drivers, all armed, provided security for their transportation. They knew the death squad was here too, but it would take time to flush them out. They weren't going to bring the trucks to the plane until the enemy had been blasted out of existence.

They would not be taking prisoners.

Scott had not examined the exterior of the plane in any detail during his and Beth's escape, but as he viewed it now, even at a distance, he figured the odds of the crates' survival were good. The fuselage was mostly intact, especially the section behind the cockpit where the crates had been stored, and the plane hadn't caught fire or exploded after the wreck. The forest floor around the plane did not appear to have been disturbed, at least not to the level that would prove Minas' forces had arrived to take the guns and supplies first.

Something buzzed above Stiletto's head. He didn't try to swat it away. He lay flat with the AK-12 in both hands, waiting for Castillo's signal—a shrill whistle. He had three fully-loaded magazines for the AK-12, and freshly loaded mags for the Colt .45. Stiletto wondered what was taking so long; he was eager to get into the fight but had to stifle his opinion. Castillo, the Venezuelan native, knew the enemy better than he did. Stiletto could best serve the unit by keeping his trap shut.

The chill on his neck told him the enemy was close.

He'd hear the signal any moment.

And then movement ahead disturbed the silence, movement near the plane, armed men rising out of the brush. They wore camouflage too, but the patches on their shoulders, black with a red X, identified them as unfriendlies. The Minas troops approached the plane, a few spreading out for security, while two more started peeking inside.

The whistle sounded, sharp and piercing.

Stiletto tightened his grip on the AK-12 and started to rise as the forest came alive with screaming rebel soldiers opening fire on the Minas troops from concealed positions. Stiletto leapt up, staying low, and ran into deeper brush ahead, to drop flat again and put the stock of the AK to his shoulder. The Minas troops in front of the DC-10 presented the easiest targets. They started to drop flat, but not before Stiletto settled his sights on one of the three, the trooper in the middle. His index finger tightened on the AK's trigger, taking up the slack, pulling a little harder before the hammer snapped home. The AK bucked, the muzzle rising as Stiletto fired a full-auto burst, but the rounds struck home, tearing open the trooper's stomach before crawling up his chest to create flower-like openings that spilled blood front and back. The trooper fell to the ground.

A second target presented itself, the man's head visible above the brush. Stiletto took careful aim and fired again, aiming low. The trooper yelled, thrashing as he fell.

Automatic weapons fire crackled all around, the rounds zipping sharply overhead. Stiletto started to crawl, rolling right, crawling some more, and rolling right again. He peeked through the brush. He was almost directly behind the DC-10. There were two Minas troopers taking cover inside, and Stiletto figured them for officers who had left their men outside while they inspected the cargo.

More gunfire, and a scream close by. One of Castillo's troopers had taken a hit. Stiletto didn't want to damage the crates in the plane, but he also didn't want to waste perfectly good targets of opportunity. He shouldered the AK again. His first burst climbed the back of one officer, throwing him hard against the interior wall of the plane before he slid to the floor.

That kill felt good.

Stiletto shifted his aim and fired again, but the second officer was gone, having run deeper into the plane, and the burst only cut through the already-damaged metal.

Another yell close by. The same trooper. Stiletto looked. The sixteen-year-old kid. He was trying to crawl out of the way of the fusillade of bullets, but his left arm, wrecked by a slug and bleeding heavily, wouldn't work. Stiletto fired a covering burst, emptying the AK before he jumped up. Slinging the rifle, he grabbed the kid under his arms and dragged him back as quickly as he could move, his boots digging into the dry dirt.

"Hang in here, kid!"

At a tree, Stiletto set the boy down and told him to lay as still as possible while he checked the wound. The kid still fidgeted but offered Stiletto a good look at his arm.

"It's not bad. Broken bone, and the slug might not have gone through," he said. "It's gonna hurt like hell, but you'll live."

The trooper didn't acknowledge, his eyes fluttering, his face twisted in a painful grimace.

Stiletto grabbed a bandage from the trooper's pack and quickly wrapped the wound, securing it with a small clip.

"Don't leave this spot," he said, shoving a new magazine into the AK-12 and running back into the fight.

He wasn't the only one on his feet now, Castillo and several more of his troopers were rushing the Minas force, their weapons spitting flame.

The Minas forces charged as well, one racing directly at Scott.

Stiletto fired, the trooper dodging to the side to avoid the muzzle flash. Scott leaped at him, swinging the butt of the AK, feeling only the swish of the swing as the trooper ducked the attempt.

Stiletto's breath rushed out of him as the trooper jabbed his belly with the barrel of the rifle he held. He doubled over, then fell to one side. As the trooper took aim, Stiletto kicked at the man's knee. The man staggered back, losing his balance and landing hard as Stiletto rolled onto his knees. The range was close, and Stiletto didn't need to aim. He extended the AK-12 as much as his arms allowed and pulled the trigger. He hosed the trooper face-to-crotch and didn't let up until the weapon clicked empty.

Movement on his left. His head snapped that way as a Minas trooper rose from the brush, having heard Stiletto's gun go silent, but he hadn't counted on Stiletto's pistol. Scott grabbed for the Colt Combat Government holstered at his hip, bringing up the muzzle to squeeze a single fat .45 ACP hollow-point into the trooper's left eye. The bullet punched the eye out the back of his head, and his lifeless corpse tumbled to the ground.

Another Minas trooper was sneaking up on a pair of Castillo's soldiers. Stiletto swung the pistol that way and let another round go. The enemy trooper arched his back as the bullet tore through him, crying out; Stiletto silenced the cry with a second round through the back of the trooper's head.

Stiletto dropped to one knee, holstering the Colt and shoving his last magazine into the AK. Time to find the second commandeering officer. He raced for the back of the DC-10.

Sergeant Mark Castillo lay flat, with the barrel of the Mosin-Nagant propped on a rock. His whistle had pierced the quiet afternoon, and as his men and the American, started firing, he took his time selecting his targets.

The Mosin-Nagant had small sights, but he'd worked with the weapon for so long that he knew how to adjust for the small notches front and back. The weapon had served the Russian army for decades and still served, not only in Venezuela, but overseas in the Middle East.

Castillo pulled the trigger. The hard-kicking slug left the barrel and flew to its target, one of the Red X troopers who didn't realize a partial tree trunk wasn't enough to protect him from the firepower of the Mosin.

The bullet ripped through the truck, continuing into the man's body. He fell and flopped on the ground. Castillo cycled the Mosin's bolt back and forward, his finger finding the trigger once again, and fired a second round. The top of the man's head exploded like a melon.

Castillo cycled the bolt and fired quickly at a pair of Red X troopers running toward his people. The knee of one exploded in a gush of blood, bone pieces flying in all directions as he face-planted in the dirt. His partner paused too long despite firing a blast of covering fire. He tried to drag his comrade to cover, but automatic weapons fire cut him down, and he fell beside his friend.

Castillo snapped his rifle to the right as more movement caught his eye, but he held his fire. Stiletto was running for the plane.

Castillo didn't know what waited inside, but the American might need help. He jumped up and ran across the field to join him.

Scott jumped through a gaping hole in the fuselage and rolled onto the floor. Two pistols shots came his way, whining off the sheet metal behind him. The enclosed space made the shots louder than normal, but Stiletto ignored the assault on his eardrums as he fired a burst, then ran for the back of a chair. The canvas seatback made for lousy cover, but he did see his target near the cockpit door, the man's black hair disheveled, his face covered in sweat.

From behind the cockpit door, the Minas trooper aimed a pistol Stiletto's way. Stiletto's trigger finger closed on the AK-12, and flame flashed from the muzzle. The officer let out a scream as the slugs punched through his body. By the time Stiletto looked up from his sights, the man was flat on the floor.

Another good kill.

But the scales weren't nearly balanced yet.

Stiletto ran out of the plane, jumping back through the hole he'd entered from, only to land steps away from a camouflaged trooper swinging a long rifle his way. Stiletto brought up the AK. At the last second, Castillo lowered his Mosin, holding up a hand and saying, "Whoa!" Stiletto moved his trigger finger away from the AK's go-button.

"Would anybody notice?" Scott said.

"I have a feeling somebody might," Castillo said. "Thought you needed help."

"I've faced worse."

The shooting started to settle down, only the occasional shot before the gunfire ceased entirely. Castillo's men started cheering. Stiletto didn't blame them. They probably felt better about the fight than he did, having a chance to avenge the family at the farm and who knew how many other victims this particular death squad had inflicted.

"Got a wounded man over by that tree," Stiletto said, pointing. "The young kid."

"Show me."

Stiletto and Castillo double-timed across the now-quiet battlefield to the tree where Stiletto had left the bandaged young fighter, who had passed out but was still breathing.

"We'll pick him up last," Castillo said. "First priority is the crates you brought."

"Let's go get 'em," Stiletto said.

They ran back to the DC-10 and the celebrating soldiers.

Castillo had not lost a single one. The victory was sweet, indeed.

But Scott knew their luck wouldn't hold forever.

Castillo rallied the troops, issuing orders to get the crates off the plane and ready for the trucks.

They had to hurry in case there was another group of Minas' soldiers nearby.

Stiletto welcomed the fight, should it come, as he scrounged the dead enemy for spare ammo for the AK-12 rifle. He was developing a fondness for the Kalashnikov; it would serve him well in the battle ahead.

CHAPTER EIGHT

Castillo's crew loaded the crates onto the trucks, and the force left the area without further incident.

Stiletto hated to leave behind the bodies of the pilots, but there was nothing else to do. Castillo said they did not have the time or space to bury them. Stiletto had collected their ID tags so their next of kin could be notified. Perhaps later, when the mission was over, he'd be able to collect the remains.

The deuce rocked back and forth once again, the truck in front loaded with crates, while Stiletto, Beth, and Castillo and his troops occupied the second. Beth, who said she had training as a field medic, took care of the wounded sixteen-year-old, cutting away the sleeve of his uniform shirt and properly treating the wound until a surgeon could dig out the slug. The kid was awake, lying on the floor of the truck with everybody else's feet up against him but still not talking.

"He hasn't spoken since his parents were murdered,"

Castillo said quietly. He and Stiletto rode near the tail-gate. Sweat had smeared most of the camo makeup on the sergeant's face, so he'd wiped it away with a rag before their departure.

"When was that?"

"Six months ago. He and his sister found one of our camps. They had their own weapons. Get this: they beat two of Minas' troops over the heads with rocks. Their clothes were covered in blood. But they got rifles that way, and found us."

"Sister still alive?"

"She is. She's very good with a knife."

Stiletto shook his head, cursing under his breath.

"It's no way to live, I agree," Castillo said.

"You're a mind reader now?"

Castillo shrugged. "We're soldiers. We think as one."

"You're awfully philosophical for a military sergeant."

"I used to teach high school," Castillo said. "Before the April Massacre."

"My briefing didn't extend that far," Stiletto said. "Can you tell me what that is?"

Castillo didn't hesitate. He explained about the protests that had turned into violence when Minas sent the military to break up the crowd.

Stiletto shook his head again. "Typical."

"Minas created many mortal enemies that day," Castillo said. "We're standing in line for a chance to kill him."

"I'm in that line now too."

"I know you are. Welcome to the club."

Castillo didn't doubt the American's commitment, even though it wasn't his fight. Castillo had worked briefly with the CIA agents sent to train the rebel army, and they'd held the same attitude. Americans had a penchant for fighting for the oppressed. Some more than others, but the ones who did show up, showed up in a big way.

The woman he wasn't sure about yet, but he'd fought beside enough señoritas to know she was probably equal to Scott on the shooting front. She was also, as he watched her care for the wounded Rico, good on the medical front.

Castillo knew the rebels needed help and he, a devout Catholic, had earnestly prayed for help. They were up against a monster and his seemingly limitless war machine. If Stiletto and Beth Carrington could provide the help that brought victory to the rebels and freedom to Venezuela, so much the better.

He had a life to get back to. Teaching was his dream, not warfare. He wanted to teach the future generation the tools they needed to avoid such horror.

He had no wife or girlfriend, but his family, living in the capital city, had not supported his decision to fight the Minas regime. His father, in particular, had wanted him to stay home and "get along" until things changed. Castillo had told the old man that nothing was going to change until the citizens of Venezuela made a change, and the only way to achieve that was by toppling the Minas government. Castillo hated the fact that the last words he had shared with his father were angry ones. The two had never argued before. But to the sergeant, there were no other alternatives.

Yeah, he had a life to get back to, a family with which to reconcile, and a future to plan.

As long as none of them ended up dead or in the hands of Minas, or in the island prison, they had a chance, and a greater chance at winning than ever before now that the Americans had joined the fight.

Castillo turned to watch the road ahead.

The two trucks picked up speed through the forest, the brush and trees getting thicker but the dirt road much more heavily packed than any Stiletto had seen so far. The ride was still rough, Stiletto and the other passengers in back jostling against each other. Beth stayed with Rico, the wounded soldier, trying to keep him stable despite the rough ride. The kid was awake now, his eyes dull, but taking the ride in stride.

Presently they passed troopers hidden off to the side of the road, who rose from cover to wave hats and yell greetings. They knew what the crates contained. By the time the trucks stopped at the edge of the camp, cheering soldiers had surrounded them. Without orders, they began unloading the crates, supporting the heavy wood containers with hands and shoulders and popping them open with crowbars.

Stiletto and Castillo jumped out of the truck. The rest of Castillo's troops followed, turning to help Beth with the wounded sixteen-year-old Rico. Castillo shouted for the doctor. Word passed from one to another, and two medics showed up to take charge of the kid.

Beth said to Castillo, "I need to see Spider's Web."

"That's our second-in-command," Castillo said. "Follow me."

Stiletto glanced back as they started forward. The rebels were doing fine with the crates, getting the guns out and passing the packages of medicine along. First part of the mission accomplished.

Second part?

To be decided.

Stiletto faced forward, with Castillo in the lead. He glanced at Beth.

"How you doing?"

"That kid took a bad hit."

"He'll make it."

"But he's sixteen," she said.

"War is hell, Beth."

Tents large and small dotted the area, the smaller tents in parallel lines. That was where the troops slept. The larger tents were mess halls, medical stations, and supply storage. It was as makeshift as it could be. There were no solid structures to see. Everything was set up to be broken down on short notice. Stiletto shook his head. The troops were eager, dedicated, and had every attribute a rebel force needed to have, and it stunned him that the stress of their living conditions hadn't worn them down more.

But when your life, the lives of your loved ones, and your country were on the line, you put up with living in a tent long-term.

Castillo brought them to a large tent at the head of the parallel rows. The occupant had tied back the flaps, his cot, small desk, and various other items on display. He stood in front of a wobbly wooden table. Stiletto spotted a book under one of the legs. The man turned their way as Castillo approached.

The sergeant stopped short of the tent and addressed the man inside.

"Sergeant Castillo reporting, Colonel."

"Welcome back. Looks like you found the supplies."

"We brought back the supplies and left behind one of Minas' death squads."

The colonel nodded. "Who are your friends?"

Castillo introduced Stiletto and Beth. Stiletto stepped forward first to shake the colonel's hand, Beth following.

"I am Colonel Ciro Verduzco, leader of this group."

"Your men fight well, Colonel," Stiletto said. "Congratulations on organizing such a dedicated force."

Verduzco's eyes seemed to fade at the compliment. Stiletto frowned. Most leaders would take such words gladly. Verduzco seemed ashamed.

"Thank you for bringing the supplies," he said instead. "With the medicine, we can help a lot of people. It hasn't been easy since the hurricane."

"I bet."

Beth jumped into the conversation. "There's more where those crates came from, Colonel."

Verduzco nodded.

"What is next for the two of you?" he said.

"That's what we need to talk about, Colonel," Stiletto said. "We aren't only here to bring guns and medicine. Minas has American agents locked up on the island prison. I'm here to get them out."

"You won't."

"My mission doesn't allow for your discouragement, Colonel. One way or another—"

Verduzco raised a hand, and Stiletto stopped talking.

"Forgive me." To Castillo, "Excuse us, Sergeant."

Castillo pivoted and walked away.

Verduzco turned back to Stiletto. "I am an awful host. Would you two like some tea?"

"Tea would be wonderful," Stiletto said.

"Yes," Beth said.

"My seating area is crude, but I'll try to make it comfortable."

"After sitting in the mud most of the day," Stiletto said, "this looks like the Ritz."

Verduzco's face remained sad. "You're being kind. Please, take a seat over here. I'll call my number two, the man you know as Spider's Web, Señorita Carrington, and get the kettle going."

The plastic folding chairs were arranged in a back corner at the edges of a ratty throw rug on the floor of the tent.

They stood as a new arrival stepped into the tent, Stiletto hunching because of the slope of the tent roof.

"This is Major Arencibia," Verduzco said.

To Beth, the major said, "You are Firefly?"

"Nice to put a face to the voice, Major." They shook hands. Beth introduced Stiletto, and the three of them sat down.

Verduzco served the steaming English Breakfast. He too had to bend down a little with the slope of the tent grabbing at his head. He sat in the last empty seat and let out a sigh.

"My men are not happy with me," the colonel said.

"I don't understand," Stiletto said.

"We have everything," the colonel said. "Everything we need to mount an assault on the capital and stage a coup. Our preferred presidential candidate is in the city standing by. Waiting. Waiting for me to call and tell him to get ready. We have the manpower, the equipment, and a plan."

"What don't you have?" Stiletto said.

"My son."

Stiletto sipped tea to give the man time to gather his next set of thoughts. Verduzco's eyes dropped, and a glance at Arencibia indicated he wasn't going to pick up the conversation.

There was nothing to do but wait. Stiletto didn't want to push. The man was in obvious pain.

It didn't take long. "My son is on the island with the CIA agents. Minas is using him as leverage against me."

"He won't be hurt as long as you cease hostilities?"

"Basically. Nobody knows but me and the major."

"How did Minas communicate this to you?"

"He released a prisoner with a coded message."

Stiletto sipped his tea and looked at Beth, who had no comment. Stiletto said, "And this is why your people are upset?"

"They know my son has been taken prisoner, but they do not know about the coded message. The soldiers will accuse me of cowardice and demand I step aside if this continues, but I can't bring myself to sacrifice my only son. I've already lost his mother."

"April Massacre?"

Verduzco nodded.

"I have an idea," Stiletto said. "Can you show me detailed pictures of this prison island?"

"I have pictures on my computer."

Verduzco handed his cup to Arencibia while he rose to retrieve a laptop from under his cot. He brought the computer back and lifted the lid, booting up the machine. Presently he turned the screen to Stiletto and showed him several color photographs.

The pictures showed a small rock off the coast of Venezuela. Calling it an island seemed a little generous, but

Stiletto wasn't going to argue the point. Obviously, one needed a boat to cross the gap between the Venezuelan shore and a wooden jetty on the prison island.

"How large a force guards the place?" Stiletto asked.

"Usually only a dozen or so. The army's misfits. They rotate every two months."

"Prisoners?"

"At least two hundred, housed in the barracks buildings here and here."

Stiletto examined each picture several times. The aerial shots were crude and really showed nothing for a proper recon. The only way to see what was happening there was to get up close.

"Sharks in the water, right?" he asked.

"And mines," Verduzco said.

"That's good. You can turn off the machine."

Verduzco closed the lid and held the computer on his lap.

Stiletto watched the man's face, but it was too hard to read. There wasn't any hope in his eyes; there wasn't sadness any longer either. Stiletto didn't want to admit that he thought he saw defeat. If that were truly the case, he'd recommend Arencibia take over immediately and damn the torpedoes, although he didn't think his opinion would carry any real weight.

What Verduzco needed was more than hope. He needed a win. But, if asked, he wouldn't know what such a win would entail, what it would look like, or if he'd even recognize it when it happened.

Stiletto knew the pain of having lost loved ones, even those that were still alive. He had the loss of a wife in common with Verduzco already, and that was enough. He wasn't also going to share in the man's grief over a lost child. Verduzco might have a better chance of being reunited with his son than Stiletto had with his daughter, but he felt he owed the man the opportunity he wasn't going to get for himself.

He said, "If I can get your son out and the other prisoners, including the Americans I was sent here to get, can you be ready to hit the capital?"

Verduzco stared blankly. Arencibia stiffened in his seat. Excitement flooded the major's face as he looked to his commanding officer for a reply.

"That's impossible," Verduzco said.

"Forget that. I got a plan. I need to see the place, and I need everything you know about the warden or whoever is in charge."

Arencibia finally spoke up. "The warden is a man named Jorge Lopez. Holds the rank of major. He's very unhappy. Minas has had him at that post for six years, and he's yet to be promoted to something better."

"Is he one of the misfits?"

"No, and that's why Lopez is so upset," the major said. "Lopez thinks he's being punished for something, but Minas won't tell him what."

"He ever leave the island?"

"Sure," the major said. "In fact, Minas' wife is having a big birthday party tomorrow night. Lopez be there. They'll all be there."

Stiletto's eyebrows popped up. "Really? Know where I can get a tux?"

CHAPTER NINE

Zurich

Harry Able sat in his office as the night crew arrived at The Trust's operations center. They came in mostly empty-handed, except for food containers. No purses, backpacks, or personal cell phones were allowed in the operations center. Every employee had a work-related cell, to be left in the building at all times unless they were conducting tasks in the field.

Most of the crew chatted quietly; some of the others, more focused, went straight to the glowing computer monitors at their workstations to begin the night's tasks.

Harry watched them through the glass wall, the lights in his office set low. None of the night crew noticed he was still there, working long past quitting time, but that didn't matter. He had in front of him a stack of paper relating to the polygraphs taken with the daytime crew. One name stood out among the others. One name that might be the mole Number One was so eager to find. The mole that had betrayed the Venezuelan mission and put the lives of Scott Stiletto and Beth Carrington in jeopardy. The results of the polygraph bothered him a great deal, and he dreaded the morning meeting with his boss, Melissa Jarrett, who would bring the big guy back to the office for his own briefing once they finished.

He sat back in his chair, and the springs squeaked. Reaching for a paper cup on his desk, he set it down upon seeing he was out of coffee. He didn't yet have the oomph required to go get more.

Because of the name.

Jenny Farnsworth was one of The Trust's longest-serving analysts. She had joined the organization about the same time as Harry and Melissa Jarrett, and she was a dedicated researcher with opinions and interpretations of information that were usually spot on. Her personnel file showed a clean background check. She'd worked for The Trust for almost ten years, and her record remained spotless.

Which was why her "indication of deception" during the polygraph test confused Harry so much.

He grabbed the stack of paper and placed them in a desk drawer, which he locked with a key. There was no sense losing any sleep over the issue, although he doubted he'd have any luck dozing off tonight. The conversation with the boss and Big Guy could wait until the next morning.

Harry grabbed his coat from the wall hook beside his door and left the office. He spent a few minutes chatting with the night supervisor, who didn't ask why he was there so late, then departed for his quiet apartment.

Stiletto marched behind Verduzco and three other rebel troops who had volunteered for a recon of the prison island.

Scott wasn't the only one using a captured Kalashnikov AK-12, so the camp armorer had provided more ammunition and several extra magazines, giving him a total of six. The mags rode in a chest rig the armorer had also provided, and the crew had found an extra set of fatigues and boots for Stiletto to wear. He felt like he was in the army again, back to basics, and the thought amused him a little. The straps on his combat harness used metal clips to hold everything together, and black duct tape now covered those clips for two reasons. One, they might make noises when silence was required. Second, they might reflect light. Either could give away their presence to the enemy. The tactic was one of the first things a raw recruit learned in advanced infantry training, and Stiletto had used up many a roll of duct tape in his military career.

The thoughts also reminded him of the difficulty of that time, when he and his wife Maddy had struggled with Army life and caring for a baby at the same time. He refused to let his mind stray too far into the past, however. He needed to focus; be in the moment. Mental distractions might cause him to miss something—signs of the enemy waiting in ambush, for example. Missing a small detail might contribute to the deaths of other rebels, or worse, his own violent demise.

Stiletto had no illusions that he was invincible. Surviving as many dangerous encounters as he had meant only one thing. He had a slightly higher skill level than any of his opponents, at least so far. Someday he might meet somebody stronger, faster, or a better shot. When he did, he knew his fight would end suddenly. He wished he might face his potential end without regrets, but he had many. What he wanted to do was live long enough to resolve those outstanding issues. Only then might he truly rest in peace.

The team moved in a classic V formation, everybody spread out to avoid two people being killed by one bullet, but close enough to communicate with hand signals. The rebels had devised their own method of communication using such signals, and Verduzco had taken time to show Stiletto what to watch for and what the signals meant. Most were basic and similar to what he'd used in the Army, a testament to the efforts of the CIA team that had worked with them previously, but other signals were not familiar. When in doubt, he was to quickly copy what everybody else was doing. Or wing it.

Verduzco raised a hand. Everybody halted, then dropped to one knee, same as the boss. The forest had been quiet except for a gentle breeze, the air still thick with heat, the canopy of trees shading them from the sun.

Now a new sound broke the silence. It wasn't loud, indicating they were still some distance away, but the sound signaled the near completion of their march and the start of the recon. The sound was that of waves crashing on a shore.

Stiletto scanned the forest looking for threats. They had to take a moment to adjust to the change in the environment and tune their senses to ignore the ambient sounds while focusing on other noises not natural to the area that might indicate danger.

Stiletto detected nothing. A glance at the other rebels and Verduzco told him he wasn't alone in that, and presently, Verduzco used another signal to get everybody back on their feet and moving forward again.

The group continued through the thick forest, stepping carefully, watching for mines or trip wires, ignoring the leaves that brushed against them. Sweat dripped into Stiletto's eyes and he wiped it away with his free left hand, always keeping his right on the grip of the AK-12, his trigger finger resting on the trigger guard. Unlike the rebel troops, he kept the selector switch on his weapon set to full auto. When the pizza hit the fan, he didn't want to spend a precious extra second fumbling with a safety catch. When the fight started, he needed to respond immediately.

Because it wasn't only his life on the line. It never was. There was always a teammate or somebody he was working to protect to think about too.

Presently they cleared the forest, and the sight before

them took Stiletto's breath away.

For a nation torn by violence and oppression, Venezuela had its places of beauty. One such place lay before them.

The ocean stretched forever, creating the illusion of peace and tranquility. The overhead sun reflected in the water, creating a shimmering effect as the waves assaulted a pristine and empty beach of white sand marked only by the usual ocean debris. Stiletto took in the sight while also looking back through the forest in yet another threat scan.

Verduzco signaled for everybody to drop flat, then snapped a finger at Stiletto and indicated he come forward. Stiletto crawled across the ground to Verduzco's side.

"There."

Verduzco didn't need to point. The object he wanted Scott to see was obvious.

The prison island where so many of Verduzco's rebels, his son, convicted felons, and the CIA team were being held sat off the coast, seemingly harmless, a circular rock with jagged edges. Waves crashed upon the sides, splashing upward in an effectual assault.

The trio of barracks housing the prisoners was obvious, as was the guard tower overlooking everything. An office building sat away from the barracks, with open space taking up the rest of the rock.

Verduzco removed a pair of binoculars from his chest

rig and passed them to Scott.

"We don't have much time," Verduzco said. "There is a helicopter patrol that covers the shoreline. They'll pass by in maybe ten minutes."

"Okay." Stiletto put the binoculars to his eyes.

The close-up view of the island didn't tell Stiletto anything he didn't already know, but the zoom did allow him to take in more detail. The wooden jetty had a motorboat moored on either side. There were two troopers in the guard tower, armed with rifles, and spotlights mounted on the rails of the tower, one aimed at the prison grounds, the other out to sea. Stiletto noticed that the light wasn't focused on the shore. He asked Verduzco why.

"They expect the mines to handle any approach from shore," the colonel said.

"Where are the mines?" Stiletto scanned the crashing waves at the bottom of the island.

"They are anchored by chains to the ocean floor, and float under the surface," Verduzco said. "They're at the right height to bump the hull of a boat."

"Can a swimmer set one off?"

"Yes. Their sensitivity is high. Every now and then, divers have to replace a mine that blows because debris, driftwood, or something else sets it off."

"Well," Stiletto said, handing back the binoculars, "it looks tough."

"Told you. You still think a raid can be successful?"

"Yes."

Verduzco remained quiet for a moment, then: "If I were going to plan the attack, I would start with mortars fired from shore. Perhaps even this spot. A barrage of them. Hit the tower, hit the main building. The prisoners who are physically able can break out of their cells and attack the guards while the assault force moves in."

"What about those mines?"

"I haven't figured that out yet. Perhaps the force pauses prior to where they've been laid and swims in. We can get equipment that will show them where the mines are."

"Do you have helicopters?"

"No," Verduzco said.

"Can you get helicopters?"

"We know where Minas keeps them, sure. Know where I can get some pilots on short notice?"

Stiletto admitted he did not. "You have no trained pilots in the rebel army?"

"Anyone with flight knowledge is either already conscripted or in there for showing rebel sympathy," Verduzco said, gesturing to the island.

Stiletto said, "Your mortar idea is a good one, and something I have in mind, too. With an added twist."

"What's your plan?"

Stiletto grinned. "Don't want to spoil it yet."

Rotor blades whipped in the distance, the sound growing as the helicopter flew closer.

"I thought you said we had ten minutes?" Stiletto said.

"My watch must be off."

Stiletto watched the helicopter fly into view. It was an American Huey, the same model that had carried to soldiers to the crash site of the DC-10 to kill Scott and Beth. The fading paint indicated the chopper had not only seen better days but was probably due for the scrap heap. But it seemed agile enough still as the pilot steered the chopper close to the shoreline and flew low, much lower than Scott figured was required for a patrol. Then the door gunner leaned out with a belt-fed machine gun, and he knew they were dropping low because he and Verduzco showed up in the target sights.

"Back!" Stiletto shouted, he and the colonel scrambling as the door gunner opened fire. The heavy machine gun chunk-chunked as solid steel projectiles rained on their position, kicking up dirt and brush and chopping through tree trunks. Stiletto covered his eyes as he moved, debris pelting his body, he and Verduzco diving for tree cover as the chopper passed overhead.

The other three rebels ran to the edge of the tree line. Verduzco shouted for them to get back, but they didn't listen. The three men shouldered their automatic rifles and opened fire on the helicopter. Scott couldn't see where the chopper was, but he also didn't think the small-arms fire would have any effect on the departing flying machine.

Verduzco shouted for a cease-fire, and this time, the rebels complied. The colonel ordered everybody to move out on the double, and Stiletto fell in behind the rebel team as they ran back along the route they had taken.

The team ran for about fifty meters, then Verduzco called a halt. The team formed a small security circle, everybody facing out, weapons ready, eyes peeled for any pursuit troops. Scott hadn't noticed a cadre on the chopper, but he wasn't about to question Verduzco's tactics. So far, the colonel had proven to know the basics quite well.

Stiletto glanced back at Verduzco, noting the concern on the man's face as he watched the forest. The breakdown in discipline meant Verduzco's ability to command was on the edge, Stiletto knew. The colonel had to do something to get the troops back in line, and fast. He knew it; Stiletto knew it. Arencibia, back at the base camp, probably knew it better than either of them. The rebels were spoiling for a fight. If they didn't get one soon, they might try something on their own and jeopardize the entire mission.

Verduzco whistled and the team fell into a V formation again, resuming the march back to their starting point, where a Jeep waited to carry them back to camp.

Verduzco drove, with Stiletto riding shotgun. The three rebel troops rode in back.

"What's your guess," Stiletto asked, "on an attack before Minas throws the birthday party for his wife?"

"Highly likely," Verduzco said. "Before we left, I asked Arencibia to contact our people in the Minas government to see if they've heard anything. We should know something by the time we get back."

The camp was a madhouse of activity as Verduzco pulled the Jeep to a stop. Troops were packing, taking down tents, and throwing equipment onto trucks. Major Arencibia rushed over as Verduzco, Stiletto, and the team hopped out.

"I talked to our people in the palace," Arencibia said. "The army has orders to hit us as hard as they can before the party, but they also want us out of sight when the United Nations team arrives."

"Okay."

"I left your tent for you to pack."

Verduzco started for his tent and Stiletto followed him, catching up with Beth along the way. She was helping to load the medical gear. He told her to save him a seat. It took ten minutes to break down Verduzco's tent and load it onto a truck, and within a half hour of their return, they were moving out with the rest of the convoy. Stiletto had no idea where they were going, but he trusted Verduzco and Arencibia to have a plan.

Stiletto and Beth sat in the back of a crowded deuce, the rough ride jostling them against each other. The other rebels, packed into every available spot, braced themselves against the bumps.

"How did it go?" Beth said.

Stiletto gave her the update, including the three troops who had fired on the chopper despite orders.

"That's not good."

"No way," he said. He raised his voice a little as he

talked about how much he liked Verduzco as a leader, hoping to plant a seed with the listening rebels that they should stay loyal and give him more time. He wasn't sure it would work, but troops in any army gossiped like schoolgirls. Word of what Stiletto had said would spread, even if they mocked him in the retelling. Somebody would agree to try to convince his mates that they should, too.

"Do you really think you can get onto that island?"

"I've never broken into a prison before, but it can't be that hard. Plus, Verduzco has almost the same plan I was thinking about. I wish he'd done something sooner, rather than hesitating."

"It's his kid," Beth said. "It's human nature. Everybody has a weakness."

"What's yours?" he said.

She blinked. "I'm not sure how to answer that."

"Good. You'll find out soon enough."

"What's yours?" she said.

"How much time do we have?"

She laughed.

"I'm counting on the warden," Stiletto said, "to have a weakness of his own."

"What if he doesn't?"

"You heard Arencibia. He's pissed at being abandoned at that position. Throw him some bait, and he'll bite."

CHAPTER TEN

The Presidential Office Center, as Minas preferred to call it, since he considered the hacienda his palace, sat dead-center in the capital city of Venezuela, surrounded by a block-wide park of green grass. No trees. Minas had ordered trees removed to prevent an assault force from having a place to hide. The guard force had a full view of the buildings surrounding the block, as well as the vehicle and pedestrian traffic. Barriers had been erected around the perimeter, but Minas saw those as a token security effort at best. A dedicated force could breach those barriers; the wide-open space leading to the main building, where an assault force would be exposed and easily cut down by the troops and heavy machine guns in front of the building, provided the true deterrent.

The domed building resembled any number of government office buildings in the United States. Minas had copied those structures because they suggested benign leadership. He had to maintain the façade that he was a man of the people. They could accept the lavishness of his personal domicile. Minas didn't think a similar center of government would be as palatable, not that he would have listened to protests anyway. But one had to give a little. Here and there.

Minas' wood-paneled office occupied the east corner of the building, its bulletproof windows overlooking the city. He sat behind his desk, dressed in a perfectly-pressed suit from Saville Row, listening to the words of General Vitorio Florez, who stood before the desk in full military uniform, his hands respectfully behind his back.

"The chopper took some fire after its pass but wasn't damaged."

Minas frowned. "It's suicide to attack the island."

"Yes, sir."

"So why are they looking at it?"

"You'll have to ask Verduzco."

Minas chuckled. "If I ever catch him, I won't take the time to ask, General."

"What do we do with the son?"

Minas shrugged.

"Are you sure you're really into this fight?"

Minas looked up sharply. "I could have you shot for asking me that."

"I don't understand why you're not taking advantage of having one of the bishops, Presidente."

"This isn't a chess game," Minas said. "One thing you need to understand. In order to have a valid hero—me, the man of the people—one must have a valid villain, and with Ciro Verduzco, we don't have to create one."

"We can't fight forever. There is the UN to consider. Verduzco may be hobbled with his kid on the island, but he's serious about the fight."

"Keeping him hobbled will give us the advantage we need," Minas said. "Time to locate their camps. Root out their spies. Wipe them out all at once when the time is right."

Florez stood impassively. Minas dropped his eyes. Yes, he could have had Florez shot for questioning him the way he had. Not disciplining the man meant the general might do some digging and discover Minas had secretly communicated with Verduzco and promised not to hurt his son as long as he stifled his warriors. And they were warriors—Minas had to admit that. The rebels could fight, and fight well, and the training from the Americans meant their skills had improved.

Minas said, "It is not for you to question my abilities or decisions in this matter. I have the entire nation to think about. The UN is going to drop a ton of money in our coffers, money that you will see a share of, General. You need to keep that in mind."

Florez nodded.

"Dismissed."

Florez snapped to attention, offered Minas a sharp salute, and marched out of the office.

Minas sat and sighed. He expected the assault planned

prior to his wife's birthday to provide high rebel casualties, which would drive them into hiding long enough for the UN inspectors to visit and provide their report to the Security Council. That would then open the flood gates of humanitarian aid. Once the UN was gone, captured son or not, Minas decided, that was when Florez and his army could satisfy their blood lust.

Minas turned his chair to look out the window. His wife's warning of the spreading rumors sprang to mind. Was Florez the source?

Minas had considered carefully what Clarissa had said regarding the rumors she'd heard of the arrangement with Verduzco. Instead of going on a tear to find out who was behind the gossip, he had decided to ignore it. One way of confirming the rumors was to react to them. If he did not react, they couldn't possibly be true.

At least, he hoped his people would view the situation that way.

The pressure of leadership was never-ending.

General Vitorio Florez walked confidently down the tiled hallway to the elevator, ignoring the civilian staffers who passed him on their way to completing various tasks.

He pressed the elevator call button and waited. Minas was wrong. If the rebels were holding back over Verduzco's captured son, now was the time to wipe them off the map and end a conflict that was costing money, lives, and material. Venezuela had very little arms production. They had to buy most of their armaments from overseas arms dealers. And that meant, sometimes, getting hand-me-down items like American Huey helicopters.

The elevator doors slid open. Florez stepped inside and pressed the button for the ground floor.

Florez knew he could run the country better than El Presidente, who was growing soft with the position, enjoying the power and luxury too much. Venezuela needed a guiding hand that didn't hesitate to stamp out trouble. The rebels were nothing but trouble, and Florez allowed a momentary fantasy to fill his mind. He saw himself and his forces destroying every rebel outpost, silencing, violently, any dissent in the streets. Only then would Venezuela prosper as he thought his country should.

Perhaps, Florez decided as the elevator deposited him on the ground floor and he walked toward the exit, the time had come to put his visions into action.

Which meant getting rid of Lazaro Minas first.

But how?

Zurich

Harry Able had spent so much time in his office at The Trust operations center, he was beginning to wonder what the sun looked like. He arrived before sunrise, and he remained after sunset.

He sat in front of Melissa Jarrett's desk in her office, with the Big Guy, Number One, seated next to him. The three were in the middle of discussing the results of the polygraph tests Harry had carried out with the staff, both day and night crews. He particularly pointed out the signs of deception showed by Jenny Farnsworth, who had an otherwise exemplary record and had been with The Trust almost as long as he and Melissa had.

Number One took in the verbal report quietly. Occasionally, he glanced at the copy Harry had provided of the actual polygraph results.

When Harry finished, the three of them remained silent for a moment.

Then Number One said, "I'm open to suggestions." His voice was low, and the closed office blocking off noise from the operations center. Even the air conditioning hummed softly.

Melissa said, "What do you think, Harry?"

Nobody wants to commit to a course of action. Harry Able said, "I think we should talk to her one-on-one. Or I should, actually, since I gave her the test. At least find out if there's any indication she might have been compromised, because I can't believe she'd betray us after so long."

"I've seen it happen," Number One said. "Usually for money."

"I checked her accounts," Harry said. "She's not had an influx of money. Her spending remains within budget, and her credit charges haven't gone up. If she's being paid for information, she's made the money disappear, and I think we can all agree that nobody who ever sold secrets for money pulled that off with any margin of success."

Number One nodded.

Melissa Jarrett watched Harry.

Number One said, "An interview is appropriate, but we need to keep the meeting private. I don't want to disturb the rest of the staff. It's critical that everybody stays on task."

"Should we give her a few days off, too?" Melissa said. "Maybe see if she runs?"

"She won't run," Harry said.

Number One raised an eyebrow. "How do you know?"

"Gut," Harry said. "She hasn't taken off since the polygraph. If she thought we were onto her, she would have run."

Number One said nothing. Harry thought he knew why. The old man knew it was possible. He didn't have the ego that allowed him to deny the obvious solution.

But the indication of deception meant Jenny Farnsworth knew something. They had to find out what.

"Is Ms. Farnsworth here now?" Number One said.

"She is," Melissa Jarrett confirmed.

"Harry," said Number One, "why don't you take her to lunch?"

"I might have a hard time with that."

"Why?"

"I haven't seen the sun in several days. I'm not sure what will happen when the light hits me."

Harry Able smiled, but neither Melissa Jarrett or Number One joined him. Their faces remained stoic, with a dash of concern.

Harry excused himself and went to find Jenny Farnsworth.

"Is this because of the polygraph?"

Contrary to his fears, Harry Able did not disintegrate when he stepped outside. He did, however, squint, so when they selected an outdoor café for their lunch and chat, Harry made sure to sit close to the wall with the overhang above blocking out direct contact with the sun. The buildings across the street partially blocked his view of the Alps in the far distance, but he at least saw the snow-spotted peaks.

"Yes," he told her.

She leaned forward with her forearms on the table. She wore a short-sleeved top and slacks, with her dark hair tied back. She had big brown eyes that seemed to fill her face. The small nose between them seemed smaller because of the illusion. "I think I know what happened."

Harry pressed his lips together. Okay, let's hear it. "Go ahead."

"I'm dating this guy named Ramon, right?"

"Sure."

"I think he might be the reason we have a problem."

Harry nodded. The waiter came for their order, but they had to ask for more time. While they consulted menus, Harry said, "Why do you think that's the case?"

"I met him a few weeks ago before we started planning for Venezuela," she said.

"You were in charge of arranging their transportation, correct?"

"Out of Miami, yes. I didn't have anything to do with the cargo."

"Right."

The waiter returned, and they ordered food and something to drink other than ice water.

Harry said, "Has he taken any interest in your work?"

"I gave him the standard cover story. I talk about the day without telling any secrets. You know, keep it to usual office stuff."

"Sure. Has he been messing with any devices you bring home?"

"Well—"

"It happens to all of us, Jenny. You throw your work cell into your purse by mistake or something like that. Did he find any work-related devices while spending time with you?"

"He might have."

"How?"

"Like you said. I tossed my work cell into my purse by accident when I was leaving in a hurry one day. I had it in my hand prior, and I was on auto-pilot because I had plans to see him."

"Did you text him or something on the phone?"

She nodded.

"Okay." If the new boyfriend was how information on the flight plan had reached Venezuela, his access to her work cell via the phone number attached to the text message would have been all a good hacker needed to work his way into the device.

And if Ramon found the cell phone later in her purse, he might have monkeyed with the device at her apartment.

Of course, he'd have needed to know what the phone was used for. Perhaps he had bugged both phones.

Harry focused his mind back on the woman before him. The technical investigation he would leave to the appropriate experts in The Trust's employ.

He continued. "When did you think he might be responsible?"

"Because one, I realized what I'd done wrong. Two, then I heard the news about the DC-10 getting shot out of the sky." She kept her voice low despite the traffic sounds and voices of other patrons. "I started to get worried, because what if?"

"Uh-huh."

"I screwed up, didn't I?"

Harry took a deep breath. "So far, all we know is that you accidentally brought a work device home. While that is a breach of protocol, it's not the end of the world."

"Still—"

"If he somehow hacked your phone and reversed the microphone to listen in on our plans, then, yeah, you screwed up, and that is a big deal."

"But how—"

"Right," Harry said, guessing her question. "How did he know to pick you? How did he know about our work? How did he know we were the organization moving supplies into Venezuela? There are more questions here than how they knew about the DC-10."

"It makes me think I might be wrong."

"It makes me think you might be wrong, too. All that means is that we have to dig into this a lot more than we thought we might."

She nodded.

"Are you still seeing Ramon?"

"Yes."

"He hasn't gone ghost or anything since the plane incident?"

"Well—"

"Tell me."

"He had to leave the country a few days ago. He's back now."

"Did he tell you where he was going?"

She looked sheepish. She said, "New York."

"Really? Around the same time that Lazaro Minas was speaking at the UN?"

She nodded.

A sense of excitement rose in Harry Able's chest. This Ramon fellow sure sounded like a good suspect, but he still had to keep an open mind. Did Jenny truly not see how he had used her, or was she a willing accomplice after all and trying to keep herself out of trouble? The only way to find out would be to give her a little rope and, of course, put a team on hunky Ramon.

"Okay," Harry said. "We're going to need to know where he lives, and anything else you know about him."

"I'll tell you everything by the time we're done with lunch."

"Good."

"You're thinking full surveillance?"

"Yes."

Her face brightened. "I'll keep him on the hook as long as I can."

Harry returned her smile weakly. Unless Number One was feeling particularly generous, and perhaps depending on the outcome of the investigation, Jenny Farnsworth would be out of a job very soon. The Trust wasn't a government entity that could put her in prison. The punishments available were slim, but they could make sure she never set foot in another government office anywhere in the world. There were some things they could do.

But that wasn't for him to worry about right now.

The waiter came back with their food.

CHAPTER ELEVEN

It was too nice a day to throw a man to the sharks.

But what was a prison warden to do?

Jorge Lopez stood at the top edge of his prison island, the open area beyond the barracks overgrown with grass, looking at the vast blue ocean and the churning waves. He glanced below. The rock face of the island and the waves crashing against that which shall not be moved looked more violent than the man-eating finned creatures lurking in wait for flesh. If those beasts failed, there were always the mines. And if a prisoner was lucky enough to survive both, perhaps he might swim to shore and win his freedom.

Lopez turned as the sound of a struggle and shuffling footsteps intruded on the reverie. Two of his soldiers, minus their rifles but still wearing side arms, carried between them a prisoner sentenced to death for murder. Lopez wished the man were one of the rebels in his custody. The man actually had nothing to do with the rebel movement, but had killed a shopkeeper while trying to rob him.

The man between the soldiers seemed barely alive, his head hanging down, his shoulders hunched, his limbs thin and showing muscles and veins. His hair was a dried mess of curls, resembling a dirty dish rag on top of his head.

Lopez didn't care what the man's name was. His shirt identified him as #45928.

The troopers brought the prisoner within two feet of Lopez, and the warden said, "Look at me, prisoner."

The man's head did not come up.

Lopez grabbed a handful of disgusting hair. He'd need more than soap and water to clean his hand. He lifted the prisoner's head so he was able to look into the man's eyes.

"Today is the day of your execution, prisoner. But, as always, I am happy to give a condemned man a chance at life."

The prisoner blinked, his face blank of any other expression.

"Down below, you see the ocean. In the ocean, we have sharks. They surround this island because they know food in the form of people is dropped from this cliff from time to time."

The prisoner showed no reaction. The wind moved some of the curls on his head, but the rest remained stiff.

"We are going to throw you into the water," Lopez said. "If you do not get eaten by the sharks, and you make it past the mines without setting one off, you may attempt to swim to shore. If you reach the shore, you are a free man. That is the word of El Presidente, not me, by the way. I only do what our humble leader says. If you reach the shore, you may start your new life. But don't murder more shopkeepers, because you won't get a second chance."

The prisoner swallowed. His eyes came alive, his breathing steadier than before.

"Are you ready?"

He gave a barely perceptible nod, but it was enough for Lopez to step aside, let his troopers push the man to the very edge of the top, and shove.

It was a long way down, and the prisoner's arms flailed as he fell through space. He screamed, but the crashing waves drowned out the noise, and then his body disappeared below the ocean's surface.

Lopez watched without emotion. Part of him wished the man good luck; the other hoped the sharks enjoyed their meal. He glanced at the two troopers. They were watching, too. He knew the men placed friendly wagers on whether prisoners tossed off the roof would survive or not. He allowed the activity. What he didn't do was try to get in on the action. All leaders, even lowly prison wardens such as himself, had to set a good example for the troops.

Miquel Herencia screamed louder than he thought possible.

The rush of air flying past him actually invigorated his weakened bones and filled his spirit with a sense of hope. He'd heard rumors of the warden's "game of chance," but nobody ever came back to actually confirm the activity. But here he was, on his way down, the ocean rushing at him faster than he'd ever thought possible, and he had his chance. His chance to be a free man again.

He hadn't wanted to stab the shopkeeper with a crudely sharpened screwdriver. All he'd wanted was a loaf of bread for his starving family. Conditions in Venezuela were such that one had to survive however possible, and, with no work and no prospect of it, Miguel Herencia did the only thing that came to mind. His family needed to eat, so he went out to steal some bread. The shopkeeper caught him, and Miguel stabbed the man. The police eventually arrested him, but only after the bread had been consumed.

With a vision of his family centered in his mind, Miguel traded his scream for a deep breath and plunged into the icy water.

Miguel didn't fight as his body sank beneath the waves. He knew how to swim; had learned as a boy. He let his body drop, and when he stopped dropping, he began kicking and moving his arms to get his body to the surface.

He broke through the frothy waves and sucked in some more air, and a little salt water, too, but that was to be expected, and he didn't try to avoid the intrusion.

Miguel then began a furious breaststroke, charging

through the onslaught of the waves, ignoring the chill that bit through every inch of his thin body.

Sharks.

There was no way to avoid the sharks. If they saw him, he was doomed. His only chance was that they were elsewhere, looking for a more reliable food source.

Mines.

Miguel didn't know where the mines were, either. He also didn't know their sensitivity but knew they went off now and then because of debris tossed around by the ocean. He probably didn't need to worry about them at all. The mines were for boats and thus set too low for a mere swimmer to interfere.

He swam hard, ever forward, the stubborn waves forcing him back. He sucked air as much as possible, trying not to cough when too much water entered his mouth. Better to swallow and carry on. Once on land, it wouldn't matter. The hardship of the swim would vanish as if it had never happened.

The next wave hit hard. Water went into his nose and mouth, and Miguel had no choice but to retch and cough. He stopped, fighting to stay above the surface of the water, let the spasm pass. Then he twisted his body and dived, kicking and sweeping with his arms, heading as far under the waves as he could. If the waves insisted on fighting him, he'd go below, only coming up briefly for more air. His energy surged as the sure-fire strategy filled his mind.

He swam with his eyes closed, keeping a vision of the

shore fixed in his mind. He could correct his direction each time he slipped above the surface.

He pushed his arms out, bring them swiftly to his side, kicking and moving forward.

He pushed his arms out again and struck something hard.

Miguel Herencia didn't have time to think about the object.

The explosion blasted a geyser of water into the air, the low boom rolling across the ocean's surface.

"Poor bastard," Warden Jorge Lopez muttered, making the sign of the cross over his chest. "Well, he died trying." He laughed. He ignored his men as he walked back across the field. Let the troopers work out who owed what to whom and how much. He didn't need to see the transaction.

He climbed the steps back to the second floor of the office building, where he had a personal work area that provided a view of the ocean, and stood in front of the pane, looking out. Lopez found his role at the prison increasingly disagreeable, to the point where he wondered what he'd done to earn the disfavor of El Presidente. He simply had no idea what he might have done to upset Minas.

He wanted to be more than a warden. Housing Venezuela's enemies was not a fun job, nor was living on the island two weeks at a time before getting on a slow boat to shore for a few days' leave. He might have been the warden, but he felt like a prisoner. The only difference seemed to be that there was nobody waiting to throw him off the roof.

There was one way to feel better, however.

Make others feel worse.

Which meant it was time to beat the Americans some more.

With a sigh, he turned from the ocean view and left the office once again.

Carlos Verduzco woke up when he heard screaming.

He didn't need to leave his cot to know who was being dragged out of the neighboring cell.

The Americans.

But he slowly rolled from the cot anyway, and shuffled to the cold steel door of his cell. Through the small window, he watched four soldiers carrying the three still-living Americans from their cells. The US CIA agents weren't moving under their own power, their feet literally dragging on the ground. They'd long since lost their combat boots, and the fatigues they'd arrived in had been replaced with the gray jumpsuits all prisoners wore. Carlos leaned heavily against the door and watched as the Americans and the soldiers turned a corner at the end of the hall and disappeared, the only remaining evidence of them another yell or two as the spies tried in vain to resist.

He turned his back to the door and slid to the floor. The smooth surface of the steel door did not impede the slide, and he finally came to rest with his bottom of the floor. He sat in a daze. He, unlike any of the other prisoners, was never beaten, just perpetually locked in his cell. He was needed as a bargaining chip, and they couldn't bargain with a dead man or one damaged beyond usefulness.

He had hoped, with the arrival of the Americans several months back, that they might help the rebels turn the tide of the war and finally get rid of Minas. His father had a solid plan for taking over the government. He'd been eager to see the plan put into motion, that he might finally see Venezuela free of the Minas scourge. But then he'd been captured. So far, his father was not only not carrying out the plan, but from what the warden had told him, not fighting at all. Because his son was locked in a cell. Which meant, the warden said—because verbal torture wasn't forbidden—that his father was a coward, a failure, and certain to let his son die while he figured out how to surrender the entire rebel army.

He breathed heavily as he sat, and groggily began a slow crawl across the floor to the cot, which he rolled up onto and lay flat on his back. He shivered. The cell was perpetually chilly, and his threadbare uniform was no defense. He'd long since given up the fight to stay warm, leaving the solo blanket provided by the warden on the ground. It was useless.

Carlos Verduzco has been too young to fight right after the April Massacre that had claimed his mother's life, and his father had sent him away for safekeeping while he joined the rebels and began the campaign to knock over the government of Lazaro Minas. Carlos had only had to wait two years before he was old enough to fight, and he took to the war like a bird to flight, racking up a kill count higher than his father's. It didn't make him feel any better over the loss of his mother; the pain from her death was too deep. But he did feel a little better knowing that Minas' regime wouldn't exist much longer. That when the rebels took over and changed the government, the people of Venezuela could live in freedom and experience true peace, free elections, and prosperity. Venezuela certainly had enough exploitable resources to fuel an economic boom the likes of which Central America had never seen.

But then Minas' soldiers had captured him.

As well as the Americans sent to train the rebels.

And then his father had lost the will to fight.

Carlos Verduzco stared at the rock above and wondered if it had all been a waste of time.

There was no way off the island.

Nobody coming to save him.

He'd die in the cell one way or another.

CIA agent Tim Pierce had no strength to resist as the soldiers dropped him into a chair and wrapped a rope around his torso several times before tying a knot behind him.

One soldier grabbed the hair on the back of his head and held his head up while his two surviving associates, Townsend and Powell, had shackles attached to their wrists prior to being hoisted off the floor and hung on hooks in the ceiling like sides of beef. The two men dangled about a foot off the ground, their bodies entirely slack, their blood-crusted faces blank. Their eyes moved a little, but the fight had left them long ago.

The beatings had been hourly when they were first brought to the island prison, then daily, then what Pierce perceived as every other day. It was hard to keep track of time with no sense of day or night, but he tried.

The door to the room opened, and the warden stepped inside. He pulled the door shut and addressed Pierce directly, not bothering to look at Townsend and Powell hanging from hooks in the ceiling.

"Mr. Pierce," Warden Lopez said, his hands behind his back, a slight smile on his face, "this is what happens when Americans meddle in the affairs of nations who desire no such interference."

Pierce, breathing hard, didn't answer. He had no strength to talk anyway.

"Very soon we will tire of these beatings," Lopez continued. "When we get tired, that's when you'll be dragged through the streets of Venezuela's capital for the world to see. We will display America's arrogance to the rest of the world. How will that feel?"

Pierce stared past the man. The words barely registered anyway. The warden was talking just to talk.

Warden Lopez snapped his fingers, and the soldiers who'd brought the agents into the cell began taking turns striking Townsend and Powell with their fists. The two agents hung from the ceiling and took the blows without any reaction. They were beyond reacting to the attacks. It almost didn't make any difference any longer.

Pierce sat strapped to his chair, knowing he'd be next, but also that the warden figured that Pierce watching his men being beaten tortured him too, in a way.

He was half-right.

Part of Pierce's mind hoped they could rebuild some strength for the moment, should it ever arrive, they had a chance to break free. Lopez's talk about dragging them through the streets was baloney. No way that would happen. Pierce knew all about Minas' visit with the UN. The information had been communicated to him during one of his routine check-ins with headquarters. But he didn't want the warden to know he knew. He wanted the warden to keep thinking his crap talk was working.

Pierce had enough wearing him down. He didn't need to listen to worthless words.

Zurich

Talk about drawing the short straw.

Harry Able sat in his car while Jenny Farnsworth and her boyfriend, Ramon Salazar, ate in one of Zurich's finer restaurants. He sipped the remains of a fast-food soda, having left a hamburger wrapper on the passenger seat of his car.

It wasn't a terribly comfortable car to spend a lot of time in, either. The Honda Civic had been built for economy of travel, not long-term surveillance. His legs felt stiff, and there was hardly any room under the dash to allow him a proper stretch. He could exit the car for the purpose, but that would only draw suspicion. He felt like a target already, wondering if Ramon Salazar had his own counter-intelligence team keeping tabs on him and the woman in case somebody, like Harry Able, was tracking them. Harry's back-up team did not report any individuals who fit the description, so he was probably okay, but he still didn't feel right about stepping out of the car, only to get back in and remain parked.

He didn't even want the surveillance job. The Trust had people for that who were trained experts and knew all the tricks. But Melissa Jarrett, Harry's boss, and the big guy, Melissa's boss, had insisted. They wanted an extra pair of eyes on Jenny and Ramon to help provide information that the surveillance team might not be looking for.

To Harry, it was a lousy assignment that had to be done. At least he had finagled a day off out of it, but not the next day. That was when he had to report on what he witnessed. At best he'd get to sleep in an extra hour. Maybe.

Jenny and Ramon weren't even sitting near the restaurant's front windows. They were somewhere in the back. Harry sat in the parking lot, staring at the front door.

Why couldn't he have been a dentist? He'd already accepted the fact that sitting at a desk and analyzing information was nothing like what he saw in the movies. Sitting alone in a car, eating rubbish and spying on two people having a date when he hadn't been out with a woman or even the guys in such a long time he wondered if his buddies would even recognize him, or if he could still properly flirt with a young lady, added insult to injury.

At least he didn't have to pee.

Yet.

His goal tonight, and the goal of the surveillance team, was to get a picture of Ramon. They'd discussed the idea with Jenny Farnsworth, and she had added further fuel to the fire of suspicions when Ramon had refused to even take a selfie with her during a date. His Facebook profile picture was a cat, and not even his own cat, the image clipped from an ad. He'd also uploaded no other photos to the social media site. The man didn't want to be identified via the high-tech means available to The Trust.

That had to change. What they wanted was to run his image through the database and see if he matched any known Venezuelan Lazaro Minas thugs.

Another two hours passed, and then Harry grabbed for the Canon EOS-1D on the passenger seat. The digital camera was set for low light, and Harry zoomed in on the door as Jenny and Ramon stepped out onto the parking lot's blacktop. From there, it was a short walk to Ramon's 435i, and Harry snapped as many pictures as the Canon could cycle. He hoped the surveillance team was getting shots from their positions as well.

Harry put the camera down and let out a breath. All that waiting for ten seconds' worth of work, and his snaps were only backups, considering the surveillance team had probably obtained their shots earlier in the evening. Worst case, they had a whole bunch to select the best shots from. Nothing wrong with that.

Harry waited for Ramon and Jenny to leave, then started his car and headed for home. He wanted out of the car, out of his clothes, and into a hot shower before he considered anything else.

CHAPTER TWELVE

The back door protested with squeaky hinges.

Stiletto followed Verduzco through the dank doorway, quickly glancing behind him, scanning the alley behind them one last time.

The door shut and left them in darkness.

An overhead light snapped on.

"Who's your friend?" a woman asked.

She stood at the end of the narrow hallway. Her small face was framed by a cascade of long black hair.

"I told Santiago about him," Verduzco said. "He has—"

"Santiago was picked up last night." The woman's eyes bored into both Verduzco and Stiletto, but especially Scott. He knew the look of somebody willing to kill, and death lust was written all over her face. She wouldn't make the kill out of self-defense, but pure vengeance.

"I didn't know, Rosita," Verduzco said.

"Tell me who this man is."

"He's an American. He's here to help. He's the one the tuxedo is for."

The woman blinked, and the look on her face softened. "I have it. Follow me."

Stiletto let out a breath he hadn't realized he was holding. Verduzco moved forward, Stiletto right behind him. The floorboards creaked beneath their feet.

At the other end of the hallway was a clothing store, most of the display mannequins bare, the shelves containing the bare minimum. The woman took them to a back room, where a perfectly-pressed tuxedo hung from a hook on a wall. The woman took it down and pushed it at Stiletto's chest. Scott grasped it.

"Whatever you need this for, I hope it helps you kill Minas," she said.

"I'll do everything I can."

"That's not enough."

"Rosita—" Verduzco began.

She cut him off. "And you! What are you doing, pretending to be a Boy Scout?"

Verduzco said nothing. Shame crossed his face.

"Answer me! There was supposed to be a 'big strike.' We're still waiting. What are you doing?"

"We need to go," Stiletto said.

"Yes, go! Run away!" The woman shouted as she rushed to the front of the store. Verduzco gestured for Stiletto to follow. The woman was still yelling obscenities when she turned from the counter and put an envelope in Stiletto's hand. The two men left the way they had come in, back into the alley. The Jeep they'd arrived in remained parked curbside, and Verduzco climbed behind the wheel. Stiletto folded the tux into a cardboard box in the rear seat. They didn't want to be seen driving around with the outfit. The sight alone would get them pulled over by Minas' security forces. The uniformed thugs covered the streets like cockroaches.

He climbed into the passenger seat and opened the envelope the woman had handed him. It was a perfectly forged invitation to Mrs. Minas' birthday party. He returned the card to the envelope and stowed it inside his jacket.

Verduzco put on sunglasses and started driving.

Scott hadn't wanted the rebel leader to accompany him into Caracas. His face was too well known. But there'd also been no choice. Santiago, the tailor, wouldn't have spoken to anybody else because of his fears of being arrested for helping the rebels. And now it was too late for a man Stiletto had never met, but felt like he owed more than he could ever repay.

Neither men spoke as Verduzco drove. Slowly, because most of the traffic consisted of people on bicycles or slow-moving scooters. More people lined the storefronts and sidewalks, going about their lives, but their faces betraying an underlying dread that had nothing to do with the still-present hurricane damage.

Stiletto again mentally affirmed that no matter the cost,

Minas had to die.

"Promise me your plan will work," Verduzco said once they'd cleared the city and hit the two-lane road out of the city.

"It will work."

It has to work. This terror has to end.

"Santiago was that woman's husband?" Scott asked.

"That's right."

"Where would they take him?"

"City jail to start. Throw him in a cell. Depends on what they wanted him for."

"What does he know?"

"Not enough to be a threat to us directly," Verduzco said. "But he might tell how he helped other rebels get into and out of the city undetected. He was our go-between for meetings in the city with the political factions who will take over once Minas is gone. Our routes in and out will be useless. He also knew the forger who made your invitation."

"Can you tell your presidential candidate what happened?"

"I have no way of reaching him without Santiago," Verduzco said. "Our people in the city will have to sound the alarm and move him elsewhere if necessary."

"Add the jail to your list of targets."

"Already done," Verduzco said. "I'll make it official when we get back to the camp."

Stiletto looked ahead. A gap between buildings allowed him to see into the mountains, the lower hills outside the city that were decorated a lush green. He frowned as he saw a structure in a clearing surrounded by a wall. Other details were too small to make out at this distance, but the structure looked like a large V.

"What is that up there?" Stiletto asked the colonel.

"That's where you're going. That's the presidential palace."

Stiletto wasn't worried about being the only white man at the party.

Rumors had reached the camp prior to the departure of Stiletto and Verduzco to the capital city that a large number of foreigners had arrived at Simón Bolívar International Airport, all of whom were being put up at the lavish government hotel Minas reserved for visiting dignitaries. To Stiletto, it proved Number One's earlier remarks about Minas opening the country to the global criminal element true, and that Mrs. Minas' party was also a cover for Minas to do some wheeling and dealing with gangsters.

Which meant that as Stiletto approached the gates of the Minas estate in a limousine "borrowed" by the rebels, he had no trouble handing over his invitation to the armed guards at the gate. There were three total, but only two were armed. The guard checking invitations wore no weapons. His two partners carried locked and loaded automatic weapons.

Stiletto had left his pistol behind with Beth Carrington. Despite the well-fitting tux, he felt naked going into the dragon's lair without a lance.

Because Stiletto had held back from Verduzco a piece of information he didn't think the rebel leader required.

The assassin he and Beth had tangled with in Miami would probably be at the party. He'd for sure recognize Scott and want a rematch.

Part of Stiletto's plan required such a development.

But it was risky. Stiletto needed a way onto the island, and the best way to get there was to be found by the man originally sent to kill him and Beth. It would have been smarter to kill the man when he'd had the chance, but the ramifications of a dead body being found at a school wasn't a complication Stiletto wanted. Scott simply had to make sure he didn't end up dead when he and the killer met a second time.

Other than that, it should be an easy night.

The guard spotted Stiletto's wry smile and frowned. He handed back the invitation and told the driver to continue to the front of the house, where a line of other cars waited, marked by their bright brake lights as each partygoer waited for his or her turn to exit. Party attendants would direct him to the festivities.

Stiletto said thank you and sat back as the driver continued on. The driver glanced in the rearview mirror and said, "Good luck, amigo."

Stiletto grinned. He didn't believe in luck. Somebody who needed luck didn't plan for every eventuality and had no way of adapting to unforeseen obstacles. Focus, attention to detail, and a willingness to roll with the punches would get Stiletto through tonight.

But he didn't want to lecture the driver on his attitude. There was no need for that. The fellow was only being encouraging in a trying moment.

"Good luck to us all," Stiletto echoed, adding, "Hey, I didn't get your name."

The driver smiled in the rearview mirror. "Paco."

Scott flexed his fingers and cracked his knuckles. His fists were the only weapons he had. He hoped they'd be enough.

Paco stopped the limo where directed and a hostess opened the door. Stiletto said, "See you soon, Paco," and exited.

When Stiletto's limousine reached the front of the line, a dark-skinned young woman in a white dress with long black hair opened the door and smiled the whitest smile Stiletto had seen in a long time.

"Welcome to the party," she said in English without an accent.

Stiletto stepped out of the limo. It was a warm night, and he let the woman lead him past the wide end of the V. Stiletto noted the open courtyard and center water fountain as the woman led him down a stone pathway alongside the building to a gate where two guards in tuxedos, their jackets yellow, stood. Beyond was the party, the pool, the fun. The woman announced Stiletto's name, and one of the guards opened the gate. The woman told Stiletto to enjoy himself. She had to raise her voice over the music coming from the rear of the house.

Stiletto followed the path beyond the gate, the V formation of the building growing more ridiculous. Was there a reason Minas had chosen this design? What strategic advantage did he hope to gain by the shape?

The answer quickly dawned on him. The building represented the "V for Victory." The palace was Minas' middle finger to his political opponents, the dissenters, and whoever else pissed him off. The building was a constant reminder of who was in charge of Venezuela and, if he had his way, who would always be in charge. The estate was visible from the city, so the population saw it every day, and didn't forget what it stood for. Stiletto hated Minas even more.

But he'd designed the two-story building not simply with an odd shape, but an outside that resembled a cheap motel.

The two floors were easy to distinguish. The ground floor walkway ended at the grass Stiletto walked across, the second level directly above, with a long rail to keep anybody on the second floor from falling to the ground. Fair enough. The doors to various rooms, offices, whatever Minas had the spaces designated for, opened outward. The place looked like a Motel 6, except they didn't leave the light on, and weren't as hospitable if you had the wrong thoughts bouncing between your ears.

He stopped to take in the sight ahead.

Beyond the point of the V, the ground began a downward slope consisting of a huge patio area, swimming pool, and bright lights. The musicians on the bandstand played a jazz number, and a large group of people on the dancefloor moved with the music. Dining tables were spread throughout.

Stiletto wandered around, cruising by the buffet, blending with the huge number of people in attendance. No faces immediately jumped out at him. He figured most of the party contained Minas' government officials and their families, and special guests from within the population, perhaps people supportive of Minas who spoke for him in public. The foreign faces jumped out, for sure. They certainly did not fit. But as Stiletto spotted each one, he had to admit that most of their identities remained a mystery, too. He knew they were part of the criminal element, but not exactly how.

Passing waiters carrying trays of drinks and hors d'oeuvres moved through the party, Stiletto grabbing a glass of champagne but passing on the appetizers for now. He stopped beside a marble statue of a woman lifting her hands to the sky and scanned the sea of faces, letting the jazz music surround him. He'd enjoyed his uncle's jazz records, and had grown to appreciate the jazz sound even as his musical interests drifted to hard rock as he got older. He had enjoyed being a regular at the one jazz club in Virginia near his former home. It had provided fond memories of happier times when his father wasn't dragging him from one Army posting to another. He'd once fancied the idea of learning guitar and playing in a band of his own, but there had never been time for that. He'd learned to draw instead, and the lack of a sketch pad on this mission made him feel like he was missing a finger.

He swallowed some champagne. The warm night air made the party almost perfect, if he wasn't here to help overthrow a dictator.

And where was Minas? There didn't seem to be a table of honor for El Presidente or his American wife. If there was, Scott hadn't caught sight of it yet. Perhaps they were delaying their appearance? More likely, Minas was away making deals with the crooks that had arrived in the previous days. Stiletto was determined to get a glance at the dictator before the night ended.

Foremost in his mind was the face of the assassin he'd tangled with in Miami.

He tried to resurrect a total picture of the man's face in his mind, but only managed bits and pieces. The only time he'd had a really good look at the man was during the tussle in the bushes at the elementary school, and in low light, too. Stiletto had to trust his combat instincts in this case. He'd know the man when he saw him. If he saw him. If he was even there. Stiletto counted about nine men in military dress uniforms mixing and mingling with the guests. One, judging by the fruit salad on his jacket, had earned more medals than any other military member in attendance.

"Fancy seeing you here, Mr. Stiletto."

Stiletto's heart jumped. On his left, a woman. Tall, dark-haired, white strapless dress with a long skirt.

He grinned. He should have expected she would be here. "You look like you're getting married," he said.

"That's the most disgusting thing I've ever heard you say."

"Considering the last time we saw each other, I'm surprised I can still shock you."

Nikki Fortune grinned and offered up her own glass of champagne.

Stiletto touched his glass to hers.

"To another successful caper," she said.

"I can't wait to hear what you're up to."

Stiletto had first encountered Nikki Fortune during one of his first major freelance assignments. The pursuit of a criminal who had stolen US defense plans from a private contractor took him around the globe, including to Sicily, where he'd asked for help from Nikki and her father, Primo.

Nikki and her father ran one of the largest organized crime rings in Europe, selling everything from guns to drugs, and whatever they could squeeze a profit from in between. But Nikki Fortune had stuck with Scott through the mission and actually proved herself helpful, despite his suspicions that she was after the defense plans for her own use. When the moment of truth arrived, she'd made no move to steal the data. For that, she'd earned Stiletto's respect, at least a little. He didn't like associating with crooks, but the spy business sometimes required one to mix with those who populated the underworld.

Her real surname was Fortunado, but she called herself "Fortune" because she was chasing her own, despite the effort leading to a lot of missed opportunities and disappointments.

"I suppose you're here," she said, "to save the country from itself?"

"Something like that."

"Well, I'm part of the bad element El Presidente brought into the country," she said.

"Have you talked to him yet?"

"Oh, sure. He's taking us in groups into this big conference room upstairs. He says we can use this country as a sanctuary if we pay him one million US every year, or we can pay ten million US and not only have a sanctuary, but also have the opportunity to invest in Venezuelan mining efforts. I guess they have a lot of oil and stuff and they're broke."

"Taking the deal?"

"No, I needed to get away from my old man for a few days." She laughed.

Stiletto smiled. The "old man" was a tough bird, who moved around with the help of a cane after being shot in the right leg. He suffered no fools, but seemed to lose every argument with his hotheaded daughter.

The jazz band started playing an up-tempo number and the slow-dancers on the dance floor cleared. She downed her champagne, grabbed Stiletto's glass, and tossed what remained of his in the grass behind the statue of the woman with her hands in the air. She grabbed his hand.

"Let's dance."

As usual, around Nikki, Stiletto felt like he was caught in a typhoon. Best not to fight and enjoy the ride. As she pulled him along, he decided getting behind Nikki Fortune wasn't the worst choice he'd ever made.

The dance floor wasn't packed to capacity, but there were enough bodies that Stiletto and Nikki had to stay close, and they moved to the beat of the band.

"Seen any of Minas' other cronies yet?" Stiletto asked.

"Gawd, yes," she said. "Some general named Florez. He's a lecherous one."

"In that dress, are you surprised?"

"You should have seen the look he gave me when I arrived at the airport in a pair of skinny jeans and a t-shirt."

She explained that the "bad element" had arrived in groups, albeit unknowingly. It was the way the flights were scheduled. Florez and two of his cronies had met everybody at the airport and taken them to the government hotel via a very comfortable bus with leather seats and liquor and "all the other things a growing girl needs," and the man who was in overall charge of the army had taken an immediate liking to her. She was the youngest woman in the group, even counting the mistresses and girlfriends of the rest of the male contingent.

"You're here alone?" Stiletto said, twirling her around and taking her back in his arms. She bumped against him, her eyes alight.

"I don't need bodyguards," she said. "You know that."

Stiletto laughed.

He'd been particularly impressed with her shooting skills on more than one occasion. Nikki Fortune was a lady who would do much better for herself if she were on the "good" side.

Whatever that meant.

Because Stiletto knew that someday they might end up on opposite sides, and at the end of each other's guns.

When that happened, somebody would have to make a very hard choice.

Scott didn't want to think about who might hesitate.

Eventually, they found an empty table and a plate of appetizers. There was still no sign of Minas or his wife, for whom the party was being thrown. Why was the guest of honor absent from her own bash?

Nikki leaned forward and touched Stiletto's leg. "Should we pool our resources?"

Stiletto remained still. She was snacking on empanadas, while he didn't eat. He did have a drink in front of him, his usual Maker's Mark. Nikki had snagged another glass of champagne. Stiletto watched the bubbles in her glass. "You have no idea what I'm doing here."

"Sure, I do. You're here to slay another dragon or something. That's what you do, right?"

Stiletto shrugged.

"Seriously, maybe I can help."

"And give up your sanctuary?"

She laughed and sat back. "Scott, who needs this place? I have plenty of hiding spots. I told you, this is simply a few days away from my father."

"How's he doing?"

"Same as always. Complains about everything. We've been making a lot of money lately, though."

Stiletto made no comment. He did not like how the Fortunados made money, so he had decided not to dwell on the subject. It was a tough nut for him. They'd once come to his aid in a big way because, at the time, his enemy was their enemy too. He should have ended the association as soon as the job was done, and in a way, he had. He and Nikki hadn't spoken in months, and there had been no plans to renew contact. But seeing her now, he couldn't quite remember why he'd thought that was a good idea. And yet, of course, he could because. . .

Enough. It was the kind of rabbit hole one could fall into and never return.

She did have a point, though. With her on the "inside" of Minas' circle, she might provide certain advantages Stiletto would have had to otherwise manufacture himself, with a 50/50 chance of success. Nikki might tip the odds in his favor.

"You know you can trust me," she said.

"I know I can."

"Tell me."

Stiletto finally spotted the prison warden, Major Jorge Lopez, at a table with two young women who were laughing at his jokes. He had a drink in one hand and glassy eyes, well on his way to a good bender.

"Over your shoulder, the man with the two women."

She glanced quickly. "So?"

"That's Major Jorge Lopez. He's in charge of the prison island off the coast, but he hates the posting. He thinks Minas is mad at him for some reason."

"Is he?"

"Probably. You don't leave a guy out in the ocean for years and years if you aren't mad at him, or think he's incompetent."

"Okay," she said.

"What he needs is a feather in his cap so big that Minas has no choice but to recognize his abilities and put him in a place of honor."

"How might he accomplish that?"

"By handing over to Minas the leader of the rebels."

She raised an eyebrow and swallowed some champagne. "That sounds delicious."

"Problem is, I don't have anybody who can get close enough to suggest the idea to him."

"He'll want to know details, honey. Like how is he supposed to pull that off? And with what men?"

"Well, he might get a tip, some very accurate information, and he has enough troops on the island to pull off the capture."

"That would leave—"

"The prison virtually undefended, yes," Stiletto said. "He'll need his men to carry out the raid. They'll be more eager than he, don't worry. I need as few troops on that rock as possible."

"When you break in?"

"Something like that."

"Who's there that's worth rescuing?"

Stiletto shrugged.

She laughed and scrunched her shoulders in excitement, and for a moment, Stiletto needed to remember where her eyes were. "This one's better than the last one," she said.

"In more ways than one." Stiletto smiled.

The band stopped playing as a man in a military uniform climbed the steps to the stage. Nikki told Scott the man was General Vitorio Florez, the one with the roving eyes.

Florez spoke into the microphone.

"If we can all stand and wish the happiest of birthdays to the lady of the house, the wife of our glorious El Presidente, Mrs. Lazaro Minas herself. Clarissa!"

The jazz band struck up a chorus of "Happy Birthday" and the crowd sang, some barely on their feet, held up by companions. The good time was contagious. Even Stiletto joined in, raising his glass, getting a good look at the lady of the house as she exited the rear of the house and followed the stone path leading to the patio. The crowd parted like the Red Sea as she ascended the stage.

Her dress sparkled in the patio lights, and her blonde hair curled down her back. Scott glanced at Nikki's hairdo and definitely preferred her straighter locks, which offered a view of her slender neck.

"Thank you, thank you all for coming," she said, hand to her heart, panning the crowd with her eyes.

She doesn't know half the people here, Stiletto thought. More than half.

"I can't tell you how much it means to my husband and me for all of you to be here tonight, and all I can say is, party on!" She let out a cheer and offered the crowd an awkward fist-pump. Nobody cared. They applauded and cheered and whistled, and then the jazz band started another number that drew more people onto the dance floor.

Stiletto stood up and offered a hand to Nikki.

"One more spin."

She took his hand without comment. This time, he led

her onto the dance floor.

General Vitorio Florez kept a close eye on Clarissa Minas she made the rounds of each table and the party in general, greeting her guests and sharing a few words here and there along with her "heartfelt" thanks for their attendance.

That didn't mean he was watching stiffly, hands behind his back, at total readiness. He sipped from a champagne glass and stood casually.

He had the glass to his lips, another swallow in his mouth, when somebody tapped him on the shoulder. Florez completed his task and turned around.

Sal Parras stood there, dressed in a sharp dark suit, a line of stitches on the side of his head.

"What is it?"

"He's here," Parras said.

"Who?"

"The American from Miami."

Florez frowned. "Are you sure?"

"On the dance floor. With the woman in white."

"There are a lot of women in white," Florez said.

"The young one with the long, dark hair."

Florez looked over Parras' shoulder, which was easy to do since Parras was much shorter than Florez. Finally, he saw the couple. "The Fortunado woman."

"Whoever she is."

"It's not a good idea to kill him during the party," Florez said.

"Who wants to kill him? I'd like to drop him in the tomb, personally."

Florez nodded. "Acceptable."

"Might cause a bit of commotion, though," Parras said.

"You will not disrupt this party in any way," Florez directed, punctuating the order with the point of a finger. "He showed up in a limousine. It's out front with the rest."

"I'm picking up what you're dropping," Parras said. "Excuse me." The assassin moved away, quickly getting lost in the crowd.

Florez downed the champagne and set the glass on the nearest table, despite the foul look from the four people seated there. Florez ignored them. They were foreigners, and Minas' idea of treating them like VIPs was not a policy idea he shared. He despised the entire idea of allowing them into the country to begin with. It invited too much trouble and made it too easy for the Americans, the Russians, or any other government who wanted a beachhead into Venezuela to insert covert saboteurs.

When Florez took over, all that would change. Venezuela could survive on its own; outside dollars were not required. The only thing the country needed was a stronger hand at the controls than it had presently.

Florez continued to follow in Clarissa Minas' wake, mentally counting the days until he could erase her from existence, along with her incompetent husband.

Stiletto said he needed to leave.

"So soon?"

Their table having been taken by others, they stood in another area of the garden, outside the edge of the party.

"Get to Lopez for me," he said, after telling her where Verduzco and the rebels were currently hiding. "If I hang out any longer, they might spot me. Somebody in particular, anyway."

"You can't help but cause trouble," Nikki said.

"It's what I do best." Stiletto kissed her on the cheek. "Have a good night."

"How do I reach you?"

"Same number," he said, adding Beth Carrington's cell for a backup.

She raised an eyebrow. "You get cell service out in the jungle?"

"You'd be surprised," Stiletto said. He winked.

Without another word, nor a real good-bye, Scott Stiletto walked away.

Nikki Fortune felt strange standing around without at least a drink in her hand, so she found a waiter and grabbed another glass of champagne. It wasn't very strong. She was three glasses down and not feeling anything. Then again, she was also Italian. She could win more fights and drink more booze before the stoutest Irishman rolled out of bed in the morning, and have a more productive day too.

She drank down the elixir in three swallows.

Now to find Warden Lopez.

CHAPTER THIRTEEN

Stiletto didn't mind changing his plan a little.

Nikki Fortune's presence in Venezuela truly was an advantage he could use, as long as Warden Jorge Lopez fell for the charade. He had a feeling the man would, and fall hard. If Stiletto had guessed correctly, he'd do anything for a chance to get off that rock.

Stiletto unbuttoned his tux jacket as he walked back around the house to the front, where the vehicles bringing party attendees had parked. Time to breathe a little easier. The plan was in motion. All he had to do now was be ready for action when Nikki called.

A small crew of Minas people remained clustered at the front of the house, the woman who had greeted him upon arrival noticing him before anybody else. Stiletto asked for his limousine. She smiled and asked a runner to fetch the proper vehicle, then stood silently while Stiletto waited.

He took a deep breath. The night was beginning to

cool; he felt the chill on his neck.

The lines of vehicles on the grass ahead seemed like a labyrinth from where he stood, but somehow the limousine he'd arrived it made the circuit up the driveway, and the woman opened the door for him to enter. She wished him a good night as he slid inside.

As soon as his rear hit the seat, Stiletto knew his entire plan had gone down the sewer.

From the seat opposite his own in the rear of the vehicle, a man sat with his hands in his lap. The limo started forward. Stiletto smiled at the assassin he'd met in Miami. The stitches on his head accounted for where Scott had smashed the barrel of the killer's FN automatic.

"Good evening," the killer said.

"I wondered when we'd meet," Stiletto said. The interior was too cramped for a prolonged fight. Whatever happened would be down and dirty, and if Stiletto won, he had the driver to contend with too. He figured Paco was dead.

"We have unfinished business," the killer said.

"Do I get a thank you for not leaving you dead in Miami?"

"You're going to wish you had."

The limo sped up as it cleared the gates of the hacienda and powered along the main road.

Parras launched himself at Scott, not only pinning him to the seat back, but hammering blows into his midsection that forced all the wind from Scott's lungs. His left arm was pinned; he struck back with his right, aiming for Parras' midsection, and the assassin grunting as the blows struck home. Parras put his knees on the seat, his bulk leaving less and less room for Stiletto to move. Parras swung his left elbow into Scott's face. The impact of the hard bone left him dizzy, and as the vehicle picked up speed, he knew he was on a one-way trip to his own death.

Zurich

"That ain't some dude she's going with," Harry Able explained to Melissa Jarrett in her office at The Trust's operations center.

Jarrett sat back in her chair, almost against the wall, as Harry Able stood in front of her desk and read from a report.

"Who is he?" she said.

"He gave his real name, Ramon Salazar. He's attached to the Venezuelan consulate in the UK. His visa information says he's in Zurich to promote investment opportunities in Venezuela, and our surveillance crew has followed him to at least one meeting, so he's making good on the cover story. His activity with Jenny Farnsworth is still a bit of a mystery."

"Does her story about the phone check out?" Melissa Jarrett said.

Harry Able turned over some pages. "Our lab went

over the phone and says that when she sent him a text, he replied back with a map link to the restaurant they were meeting at. She clicked on the link. Salazar's hacker managed to put some malware into the restaurant website, and when Jenny opened the link, bam. Right into her phone, and ultimately, our entire network."

Jarrett cursed.

"We're in the process of cleaning it up," Harry assured her.

"Too late now. Who knows who Salazar is selling the information to?"

"We're confident he isn't."

"Why?"

"He's made no contact with anybody other than business appointments and Jenny. He's only here for our Venezuela information."

"Do we know how they found out about us to begin with?"

Harry closed the file. "No."

Jarrett frowned.

Harry said, "I'm working on the theory that somebody at CIA talked once they asked us to do them the favor of bringing their guys back."

"Probable, at least. It might even explain how their agents were captured."

"But what if Jenny isn't telling us the whole story?"

"I'd hate for that to be the case."

"Same here." Harry finally sat down, leaning his elbows on his knees, and he looked Melissa Jarrett in the eye. "But we have to keep checking her out, and perhaps let her go."

"That's up to the old man."

"I understand, but he'll need your recommendation."

"I know. I'm not sure what to do yet. Has anything suspicious turned up with her?"

"Keeps coming back clean, no matter where we look."

"Somebody at CIA with a big mouth is probably our best answer, and Jenny just happened to be single."

Harry shrugged.

"Our people still on Salazar?"

"Digging deep, yeah."

"The best way to figure this out might be to grab the Latin Romeo and make him sweat a little."

"And Jenny?"

"Unfortunately. We'll need both their stories to see who's lying."

"The malware thing makes—"

"Makes me think," Melissa Jarrett said, "she accidentally used a work device for the purpose of allowing access. She might look clean because she's having him send whatever he's paying her to an account we don't know about, perhaps a relative's, or he's using cash."

Harry sighed.

"I don't like it either, Harry, but we've been doing this too long. We need to know."

"Sure."

"Is Salazar staying at a hotel?"

"Renting a home, actually."

"That's all for now."

Harry Able set the report on Jarrett's desk and left her office.

Melissa Jarrett scooted close to her desk and picked up the phone. It was time to report to Number One and get his input on the next course of action.

Might as well leave the hard decisions to the guy who ran the place.

El Presidente, Lazaro Minas, paced a small space on the deck outside his bedroom at the hacienda.

General Vitorio Florez, in full military dress, stood watching nearby.

"Who was the man?" Minas asked.

"An American."

Minas paused, scoffing. "Another American? Do they never give up?"

Florez ignored the question.

"I'm glad your people removed him without disturbing the party," Minas said. "My wife had a wonderful time."

"Of course, sir."

"My meetings went well too," Minas added. "There will be much hard cash coming into Venezuela, Vitorio."

The general nodded.

"Where is the American now?"

"The island."

"Please send word to Warden Lopez that he is to be mistreated at will."

"I don't think he'll argue, sir."

Minas stopped pacing and looked Florez in the eye.

"Something else on your mind, General?"

"Does it show?"

"You're unhappy about something. What is it?"

"There was a woman with the American," Flores said. "Nicole Fortunado."

"You think they're working together? I find that hard to believe, knowing the Fortunado reputation."

"I think we should at least question her."

"No," Minas said. "She arrived alone, so the American probably sought her out for an evening's diversion. I will not risk ruining the arrangements I've made because you're suspicious about somebody. I also do not want to earn the wrath of her father. Do you have anything else to go on, other than you saw them dancing?"

"No, sir."

"Leave her, then."

Florez nodded.

"All right, I need a drink." Minas walked past Florez into his bedroom. "That's all for now, General."

Florez walked away with his hands behind his back. The conversation only strengthened his resolve to remove El Presidente and take over. The man was not fit to lead and was leaving their country open to attack.

His incompetence had to be stopped.

"You are a very well-dressed prisoner."

"Dress to impress," Stiletto said, "like Mom used to say."

"Where is your mother?"

"Retired in Florida."

"How nice for her."

Warden Jorge Lopez nodded at the soldier beside him, who slammed the butt end of a wooden baseball bat into Stiletto's gut.

Stiletto let out a howl as his abdomen flared in pain, the muscles tightening, his body rocking back as he hung from a ceiling support beam, his wrists bound by handcuffs draped over a hook that had been anchored into the beam.

Stiletto took a breath and groaned again. He was in a cell. A bulb dangling from a wire hung near him.

"I've been told to abuse you all I want," Lopez said. "Nobody here is going to help you."

"That's okay," Stiletto said, still hurting. "This is the torture scene. I'm used to it."

"You think you're funny, don't you?"

"You want to make me talk, get out the carpet-beater. I have nightmares about carpet-beaters."

Lopez frowned. Stiletto grinned and let out a chuckle. The soldier swung the bat again, this time against Stiletto's upper right thigh. Another howl.

"Okay, that one hurt," Scott groaned.

Lopez laughed. "What am I supposed to do with you?"

"Ask your president."

"El Presidente doesn't care about us here on the rock, I assure you. We are left to rot."

"You too?"

Lopez shrugged. "I am a soldier in El Presidente's army. I follow my orders."

An idea flashed through Stiletto's mind. One that might buy him some time.

"What about what attractive women whisper in your ears, Warden? Do you follow those too?"

"What are you talking about?"

"Who do you think gave the woman her information?"

"You?"

"No, Richard Nixon! Of course, me! Idiot."

Lopez frowned. "Why would you do that? Aren't you working with the rebels?"

"Is that what El Presidente told you?"

"He only told me I was to beat you mercilessly, like the other Americans."

"Minas doesn't want to fight the rebels. He only wants a reason to stay in power, and the rebels help him do that. He wants to keep the war going in perpetuity."

"Why do you care what happens in my country?"

"I care about the money I can make, Warden. We picked you because you have enough men to pull off the job, and you certainly have the motivation. Why are you working for a man who's keeping you on this rock?"

The soldier made a move to lift the bat again, but Lopez held up a hand and he lowered the weapon.

"You may have talked your way out of a beating, for now," Lopez said, "but I'm sure we will resume once I check out the information your woman friend provided."

Stiletto dangled, still breathing hard. Had the ploy worked? He needed Lopez to act on the information he'd told Nikki Fortune to pass along. His entire plan depended on Lopez trying to eat a fish bigger than his head.

Lopez issues orders to the solider and left the room. Stiletto waited, still hanging, while the soldier made no move. Presently two more troopers arrived and helped get Stiletto unhooked. They carried him out. Stiletto let his body relax. There was no sense in fighting. The trip didn't take long. The soldier who had struck him with the baseball bat stopped in front of a barred door, which he opened using a key. The hinges screamed. The other two troopers placed Stiletto on the hard floor inside and departed. The cell door shut with finality. The click of the lock was an afterthought.

Stiletto lay still and caught his breath.

Somebody near him coughed.

Warden Jorge Lopez returned to his office and picked up the desk phone, calling for his second-in-command.

When Lieutenant Herman Martinez arrived, he and Lopez had a short conversation, which included Lopez showing Martinez a spot on a map. Martinez was to take a squad to the spot on the map and report back. Martinez agreed to the mission, but asked that the mines between the prison and the mainland be removed so he and his men could travel back and forth safely.

Lopez said, of course. What did Martinez think he was, a monster?

Stiletto painfully rolled onto his side to face the other prisoner. His body still hurt from the strikes of the baseball bat. His stomach hurt more than his leg.

The other prisoner sat in a corner, knees curled to his stomach, his arms wrapped tightly across his chest. His clothes were dirty; his face filthy.

"Hi," Stiletto said.

"Who are you?" the man said.

"I'm Scott," he said. "I'm an American. Who are you?"

"Carlos Verduzco."

A chill flashed up Stiletto's back that had nothing to do with the cold within the cell.

"Pleased to meet you," Stiletto said. He started crawling across the floor to his own corner. He didn't want Carlos to know he recognized him, or to say anything stupid like, "I'm here to get you out as soon as that fool of a warden takes the bait I've given him," because the cell might be bugged. Scott didn't think for a minute he had been thrown in the cell randomly.

"I'm going to take this corner right here," Stiletto said, and made himself small.

Carlos Verduzco said nothing. He watched Stiletto with steady eyes. The long stare almost made Scott nervous, but the American kept his mouth shut. He only had to maintain silence long enough for the plan to work. After that, he could talk until he ran out of words.

One camp was the same as another after a while.

The stress and strain of moving such a large group and maintaining contact with other such units remained the same as well.

This time it was worse, though. Stiletto hadn't been in contact for over twenty-four hours.

Colonel Ciro Verduzco wasn't sure what to do but give the American a little more time.

Major Gustavo Arencibia wasn't as convinced.

"We miscalculated," the major said. "Stiletto is either dead or captured. We need to strike without delay."

They sat in Verduzco's "new" command tent. It was the same tent as before but in a different spot in the jungle. The other tents were spread out, troops busy trying to make the camp home, while also awaiting move-out orders. The only light in the camp was from strategically placed lanterns, quick to put out in an emergency, but eerie shadows danced across the ground with the flickering lights.

Ever since Stiletto's departure, rumors had spread of the coming action, and the troops wanted action more than food and water. They wanted their country back, and would not settle for anything else.

"We know something bad happened," Arencibia said to the unresponsive Verduzco, "because Paco did not return either. Whatever happened took place once they'd left the party."

Verduzco blinked.

"We tried, Ciro. Now we need to take Minas down in memory of your son and everybody else we've lost. This waiting is pointless."

A fly buzzed around Verduzco's face. He made no move to sweep it away.

"Are you even listening to me, Colonel?" Arencibia asked.

No reply. But at least Verduzco finally waved away the fly.

"I'm listening," Verduzco finally replied.

"What are we going to do?" Arencibia said.

Verduzco started to open his mouth when somebody shouted, "Colonel!"

Verduzco and Arencibia looked outside the tent to see Beth Carrington running toward them.

It was tough finding something to do around the camp since the troops didn't want a stranger helping out with gear. Beth Carrington saw their point, in a way. It wasn't that they didn't want her around, but they were such a well-oiled machine that had moved camps again and again that she'd only gum up the works. But a patrol squad going on a march around the perimeter brought her along, and that helped get her mind off the fact that Stiletto hadn't returned from the Minas' birthday party.

Beth and the squad went around the perimeter several times, slow and steady because it was dark, watching for threats. The squad leader made scratches in a small notebook now and then, but she didn't ask what he was information he was recording. It was none of her business.

As the replacement squad came out to meet them and Beth's crew started back for the camp, her cell phone vibrated. She frowned at the unfamiliar number, but since Scott might be calling on whatever he could get his hands on, she answered.

"Hello?"

"Are you Beth?"

A woman's voice.

"Yes, this is Beth."

"We haven't met. My name is Nikki Fortune. Scott told me to call this number in case I couldn't reach him."

Beth paused; the squad glanced back at her, but she frantically waved them on. They continued into the camp.

"Why did he do that?" Beth said.

"I called his number, and somebody else answered— the warden at the prison. I recognized his voice from our conversation at the birthday party. I don't have all the details, but Scott was captured. I managed to get that much out of Lopez, but he's checking up on what I told him."

"What did Scott ask you to do, Miss Fortune?"

"Are you being funny?"

"Should I have called you Miss Bitch instead?"

The woman on the other end of the line laughed. "No, you can call me Nikki. Scott and I go way back." Nikki provided a rundown of her interaction with Scott at Minas' party, some of her background, and what she was doing in Venezuela. "He told me to call you if I couldn't reach him, and I couldn't, so I'm calling, and I'm telling you that Warden Lopez took the bait. He's going to check out the location of your camp and use his troops from the prison to make the raid to try to capture your boss, whoever that is."

Beth Carrington didn't reply right away. Nikki Fortune seemed to know the plan, but Scott had made no mention of including her in the details.

"You're a new player on the board, Miss Fortune."

"Scott wasn't expecting me either, but you spies are all about adapting and improvising and overcoming, right?"

"Something like that."

Beth started hurrying for the camp. Verduzco and Arencibia had to be told straight away.

"Can I reach you at this number, Miss Fortune?"

"Call me Nikki, goddammit!"

"Can I reach you at this number, Nikki?"

"Or my hotel." Nikki provided the name and number. Beth quickly memorized both.

"I'll get back with you, Nikki."

Nikki cursed. "I'll see what else I can find out. Maybe Minas will tell me something if I ask nicely."

"Do it. Talk soon." Beth ended the call and broke into a run for Verduzco's tent, yelling, "Colonel!" as soon as she was close enough for the man to hear.

When the single light in the cell blinked out, Carlos Verduzco told Stiletto the on and off action of the light was the only way to tell day from night.

"Lights out?" Scott said. The pitch-black in the cell was thick enough to cut. Once his eyes adjusted, there was a small glow through the barred door, from out in the hall. "Don't we get a blanket?"

"You're new here, aren't you?" Carlos asked. He let out a short laugh.

His spirit isn't broken. Good. "I don't plan to stay long, Carlos."

"Why is that?"

Before Stiletto answered, Warden Jorge Lopez stepped in front of the cell door. He put a key in the lock and opened the door himself. Stepping aside, two soldiers entered, and Lopez ordered them to pick up Stiletto. Scott didn't resist as each one took an arm and hoisted him to his feet, then partially dragged him behind Lopez as they made their way down the narrow corridor. They passed other cells, Stiletto trying to get a glimpse inside, but the soldiers blocked the view. He had a sense, passing one cell, that hot eyes were looking out at him.

Presently, the soldiers dragged Stiletto across the grassy field, up the steps to the second floor of the main building, and into Lopez's office, where they dropped him into a chair. Lopez sat down behind his desk and dismissed the troops, but told them to remain outside the door. The soldiers complied. One pulled the office door closed as he exited.

The large window in the office would have been nice during the day. Now, it looked like deep space on the other side of the glass.

"Your woman friend called," Lopez said.

"Really?"

"We recognized each other from the party. So, I am inclined to believe your story. I am sending troops out on a scouting mission in the morning to see if the camp is where you say it is."

"And if so?"

"Why are you doing this, Mr. Stiletto?"

"There's a price on my head."

"Who wants to kill you?"

"The Russians."

"For what?"

"Some murders in Moscow. A few other things."

"How much is the reward?"

"Not enough to trouble you, Warden. Besides, what could you do with it while stuck on this rock?"

"I have vacation coming up."

"No, what you want is something more than that, and we both know what it is. You've been watching Minas run your country into the ground, not deal with the rebels, and generally behave like a pig. You know you can do better."

"Do I?"

"I see it in your eyes, Warden. You were made to do more than run a prison—where you're basically a prisoner yourself, if you haven't noticed."

Lopez said nothing. He tapped his right index finger on his leg.

"Some days, it is tough running a prison," Lopez admitted.

"When your scout party reports back, you'll know I'm telling the truth."

"Do you expect me to give you asylum?"

"Sure."

"Why?"

"Do your homework. I'm a mercenary. You're going to need to rebuild the army after you take over. Who better than somebody like me, who has access to men and equipment, who can help rebuild your forces into ten times what they are now? Isn't that worth something?"

"Minas has many allies."

"You'll need people like me to keep them from taking

you out."

Lopez acknowledged that as a possibility, adding, "It would be nice to kill them first."

"I don't usually miss," Stiletto said.

"I'd expect nothing less from somebody like you," Lopez said.

"Do we have a deal?"

Lopez laughed. "Not so fast. I need to hear from my scouting party. Right now, let's say I'm leaning toward an alliance with you. I can lean the other way very quickly, and then you'll be fed to the sharks."

"It's not hard information to gather," Scott said. "What do we do in the meantime?"

"In the meantime, you will go back to your cell, you will behave yourself, and I will collect you once I hear from my scouting party."

Lopez rose from his chair and opened his office door. He ordered the troops to return Stiletto to his cell.

Scott said nothing as they hustled him out, but his mind was filled with thoughts. Especially thoughts of Nikki Fortune. Once she'd reached Lopez, she had hopefully called Beth. The plan seemed to be falling into place, but one misstep, one gap in communication, and he'd get all of his friends killed.

CHAPTER FOURTEEN

"What did this woman tell you?" Verduzco said.

Beth Carrington shared the full story of her conversation with Nikki after catching her breath and giving Verduzco and Arencibia the basics. They did not offer her a chair. She remained standing as she gave the report.

Verduzco glanced at Arencibia for comment.

The major said, "We need to put a watch on the prison right now, before the sun comes up. If Lopez takes the bait, he'll want to investigate first."

"That means sending a search party," Verduzco said.

"As soon as the sun rises."

"That also means—"

"Removing the mines. Once the scout party leaves, that will be our opportunity. Let me lead the squads. We'll start with a mortar attack, while another squad goes in on a boat."

Verduzco considered the idea quietly.

"If the scouting party leaves," the major continued,

"we need to attack."

"And if they don't?"

"Then Stiletto's dead, the plan didn't work, and we need to strike, because Lopez will still deliver information about this camp. That means we won't last much longer than the American."

Verduzco nodded. "Do it, major. Right now."

Arencibia left his chair without another word and began shouting commands.

Beth looked at the colonel. He still seemed muted and uncertain, and she felt like she had to say something to try to change that.

"Stiletto's alive," she said, "and so is your son. This is your opportunity to turn your country around."

Verduzco nodded. "I know it is. I needed somebody else to show."

Verduzco smiled. Beth almost fainted. She hadn't thought the colonel was capable of smiling.

"I've had the best help, Miss Carrington. Shall we prepare the troops for battle?"

Beth smiled too.

Major Gustavo Arencibia, flat on his belly in the thick undergrowth, pulled binoculars from his combat vest. He peered across the gap of ocean to the prison island. He'd pushed his troops hard upon leaving the camp, and every man was still catching his breath. Arencibia's legs and feet were sore.

The searchlight on the guard tower provided the only illumination, other than the bright moon, but even that light wasn't enough to get a clear picture of what was happening on the rock.

Beside him, Sergeant Castillo, with his ever-present Mosin-Nagant 91/30, the antique rifle he insisted upon carrying, asked, "Anything?"

"We won't see much until morning," the major said. "I want the mortars set up in a line and the bombs prepared. Then, split the troops. I want some on watch, and some to sleep."

"And you?"

"I'll stay on watch. You get some rest. I will wake you when I need a break."

"Yes, sir," Castillo said, backing quietly away to issue the orders.

Arencibia continued scanning as his men began setting up the mortar launchers that would pulverize the prison and enable their assault. Verduzco had not asked where they would get a boat to use in their attack, but the major knew that was a simple action. There were two boats moored to the island's jetty. The scouting party would need one to get to shore, so that boat would be waiting for them when they required the craft.

Staring through the binoculars, the major knew, was pointless, but Arencibia also didn't want to miss anything, not even one hint of activity. They were closer than ever to freeing their country and butterflies wrestled in his gut, the anticipation almost too much. Remaining still took effort. He needed to move around, expend the energy somehow, but consoled himself that the opportunity to do so would come very quickly, and when least expected.

Sergeant Castillo jabbed Arencibia in the shoulder.

"They're crossing."

Arencibia woke up instantly, grabbing his binoculars and rifle and following Castillo through the undergrowth to their look-out position. Arencibia, on his belly, peered through the binoculars once again and smiled.

"Two boats," he reported. "Twelve men."

"This looks less like a scouting crew," Castillo said, "and more like an assault force."

"They're ready to strike if they find the camp."

Arencibia pulled a handheld radio from his belt. Castillo had the same model, so the two could communicate once the action started. He pressed the Talk button.

"Overwatch to home base," he said.

It took a moment, but Verduzco's voice came back over the speaker. Despite the low volume, Arencibia heard the colonel clearly.

"Yes."

"Two boats. Twelve soldiers."

"That is more than half the company on the rock."

"I'd say so."

"We're ready for an attack."

"We're ready to strike."

"Fire away, major."

Arencibia acknowledged the order. With two fingers in his mouth, he let out a whistle. Once to his right, another to his left. The signal the mortar crews were waiting for. They'd prepare their first volley and wait for another signal to start the attack.

Arencibia gathered his men and gave them a rundown of the plan. Wait for the landing party to abandon their boats, then take the boats and attack the rock while the mortar shells fell.

As soon as the last word left the major's lips, Castillo, who had kept an eye on the boats, tapped his shoulder. Arencibia put the binoculars to his eyes once more and watched the scout troops pull the boats to the shore of the beach. They were motorboats, controlled from the rear. Easy to operate. He watched the troops run up the beach, following their commander. They were kitted out in full battle fatigues, rifles, radios, packs, the works. Once Arencibia lost sight of the force, he lowered the binoculars and exchanged looks with Castillo.

"We can take them out," the sergeant suggested.

"And lose how many in the process?"

"With my rifle? We wouldn't have to get close."

"Stand down, sergeant. Save it for the rock."

The hardest part was letting enough time go by for the

scout force to be well underway with their march to the camp.

Arencibia quieted his anxious troops each time they insisted enough minutes had passed. Arencibia kept a close eye on his watch. After thirty minutes had ticked by, he gave the order for Castillo to lead the troops to the boats. The sergeant and the rest of the rebels marched forward, heading for the path that would lead them to the sandy shore. Arencibia whistled twice more and followed them.

By the time the troops hit the sand and broke into a sprint for the abandoned motorboats, the mortar tubes began belching death. With two troops each operating three tubes, the rain of hell on the rock would be merciless.

Arencibia didn't need to see the bomb strikes on the rock. He heard them, the thundering booms stretching across the water. He jumped into one boat with part of his force, Castillo the other with those remaining, with one soldier for each boat pushing the crafts back into the water before jumping aboard. Arencibia and Castillo fired up the engines and steered for the rock at full speed as mortar shells continued passing overhead, smashing into the rock with enough finality that the major wondered what would remain when they arrived.

The guard tower fell into the water, the troops stationed at the top vanishing beneath the surface of the ocean. More explosions burst across the field, striking the troop's barracks and rattling the main building. The boats closed the distance quickly, Arencibia and Castillo steering for the jetty that would allow full access to the prison structures.

Ocean spray blasted Arencibia's face, but he made no move to clear the water. His troops held up their free arms to block the assault. He slowed his boat to allow Castillo to land first. The mortar assault ceased. Arencibia cut the motor, but his boat still bumped into the jetty. One of Castillo's men threw a rope, jumped off the boat, and tied the craft to the jetty. Castillo led his crew onto the rock, his antique rifle at the ready, the other troops with their automatic rifles already scanning for targets.

Arencibia gave the boat enough gas to get them to the jetty, and his troops didn't wait for orders. They leaped out, running after their comrades. Arencibia joined the rush, unconsciously flicking off the safety on his rifle.

Troops swarmed at them from around the main building, automatic weapons chattering, Arencibia's troops hitting the ground and rolling as the bullets zipped through the air. Arencibia landed hard in the grass, firing, his US M-4 carbine bucking against his shoulder. He liked the new weapons supplied by the Americans since he had no worry about worn out parts breaking in the middle of combat. He tracked a guard as the man jumped up and ran for another position, his burst cutting down the guard halfway there. The man tumbled into the grass and lay still. Some of his men tossed grenades. The resulting blasts rocked the ground, tearing apart more guards. He jumped up and shouted for his men to charge. The force ran into the drifting smoke left behind by the grenades, firing at any stragglers they saw—the prison forces not killed by the grenades woozily making for new positions to fight. They all fell to rebel bullets.

"What's that?" Carlos Verduzco said, finally leaving his corner to stand. The explosions were unmistakable. The walls and floor vibrated with each impact. There were no windows to look out of, but Stiletto grinned. He knew. Right on time, Colonel.

"We're getting you out of here, Carlos. Your father sent me."

Carlos snapped his attention to Scott. "My father?"

"I'm sure he sent Major Arencibia to do the honors. Unfortunately, I'm a little tied up at the moment."

"There are other Americans—"

"Yeah, I'm supposed to take them too."

"If they're still alive."

More thundering blasts.

"That's what I'm afraid of," Stiletto said. "Where are they?"

"Two cells down. One was brought in dead, and they threw the body to the sharks. Another died from the beatings. They threw him in the ocean too. The other two are still alive."

The bombing stopped, and gunfire replaced the explosions. A lot of gunfire. Then, more explosions. Hand grenades, probably. Then the shooting stopped.

"Why did they stop?" Carlos said.

"Because they're on their way. Can you move me away from the door?"

Carlos Verduzco, despite his appearance, hustled. He grabbed Stiletto under each arm and pulled him out of the direct line of the cell door.

"This wait is going to be a tough one," Stiletto said. Carlos propped him against the wall not far from his former corner.

Carlos set his gaze on the cell door.

"I've been waiting a long time for this. A few more minutes won't hurt."

Arencibia directed Castillo and his crew to check the guard barracks for more troopers and to set up a security perimeter once the building was cleared. He and his squad ran for the prison barracks, the windowless building looming as they approached. The side entry wasn't armed. Arencibia opened the door and stood aside for a moment. No gunfire came their way, but a lot of men started shouting as they entered the cell block.

Cells to the left and right. Arencibia shouted for his men to drop as two prison troopers appeared in the doorway at the other end, shouldering their rifles. The weapons spat flame. Arencibia and two rebels returned a stream of full-auto fire, chopping the troopers to ribbons. The two guards fell in the doorway.

Castillo slightly modified the major's orders.

He sent half his force to the barracks as instructed, but he took two men to hit the main building. The warden was in there somewhere, and Castillo had a score to settle. They hit the first floor to start, opening fire as they entered, spraying the room. No guards. Castillo and his men checked each of the side offices but found nothing but empty desks. Outside, they started up the steps to the second floor. That was when somebody leaned out through the doorway and leveled a pistol.

Warden Lopez. Castillo would know the snake's face anywhere. The warden's pistol cracked once, the bullet zipping over Castillo's head. He shouldered his Mosin-Nagant and let a round go. All he needed was one shot. He'd had friends and relatives imprisoned on the island, but they were gone, killed long ago and tossed off the rock in one of Warden Jorge Lopez's sick games. Castillo's desire for vengeance was satisfied as Jorge Lopez's head vanished in a spray of shattered bone and brain sludge. His upper body tipped back and landed with a squish on the walkway outside his door.

But Castillo had no time to celebrate. He rushed up the steps to the body. His eyes landed on the cell phone that fell from Lopez's pocket. Ignoring the mess, Castillo grabbed the phone and looked at the last call, made only a minute before, to a phone number Castillo didn't recognize. A chill crept up his neck that had nothing to do with the cold from the rock. He told his men to set up a secure perimeter and pressed REDIAL.

Castillo wasn't worried about the cell signal not reaching the mainland. He waited for the connection, and somebody answered.

"What now?"

Castillo allowed himself a laugh. He ended the call.

He imagined that General Vitorio Florez, at the other end of the line, was quite upset.

"Choppers incoming!" he shouted to his men.

His men scrambled back the way they had come, Castillo keying his belt radio to advise Arencibia of the new development.

"Lopez sent out an alarm. We're gonna have company."

"Acknowledged. We'll have plenty of angry fighters to meet them with."

"Did you find the American?"

"Yes. You'll see him shortly."

The major stood before the cell block, stunned.

Prisoners yelled from behind their cell doors, pressed close to the steel bars, waving and shouting, their voices echoing. It was almost too much. There would be hundreds of these men, in various stages of mobility. They'd come for the colonel's son, but they couldn't refuse all the other prisoners.

Arencibia began shouting back, urging every prisoner to calm down while they figured out a way to get the cells open. He sent some men to search for a key, and presently two of the rebels came back with two sets, enabling more than one soldier to unlock doors. While the sound of squeaking hinges filled the cell block beneath the water and a mass of men filling available space, Arencibia moved down the corridors shouting for Scott Stiletto.

He found Carlos Verduzco first, who extended his arms through the barred door to get the major's attention and responded to the major's shouts that the American was in his cell.

It took a moment for the trooper with the keys to get the cell door unlocked, then Arencibia went inside. He and Carlos hugged, Carlos assuring the major he was all right, but how was his father? The major told the son that his father was well, and still leading the rebels. Stiletto did not interject. There was no point in telling Carlos about the drama leading up to his rescue.

Arencibia knelt beside Scott and examined the handcuffs. Digging through the pockets on his combat webbing, he produced a handcuff key. He expressed doubt that it would work, but Stiletto said it was worth a try. Arencibia started with Scott's wrists, giving the key a turn in the handcuff lock. The locks snapped open, and the cuffs clattered onto the ground. The major quickly removed the shackles on Scott's ankles, and Stiletto, using the major and the wall for support, rose to full height.

Scott paused for a moment, his body sore but nothing broken, a feeling of normalcy quickly taking over. He shook Carlos's hand in a proper greeting, then asked the major how they were fixed for getting out of there.

"We have a ton of men to arm," Arencibia said. "We'll find the armory and take care of that."

"How many boats did you bring?"

"We stole the two we used to get here, but there are more in a cove on the opposite side of the island."

The radio on Arencibia's belt crackled as Castillo's voice came over the speaker, echoing in the cell.

"Lopez sent out an alarm. We're gonna have company."

Arencibia removed the radio from his belt and raised it to his mouth. "Acknowledged. We'll have plenty of angry fighters to meet them with."

"Did you find the American?"

The major smiled at Scott. "Yes. You'll see him shortly."

"And Carlos?"

"He's here too."

The major put the radio away. "Let's rally the new recruits. We still have a war to win."

Scott and Carlos Verduzco followed the major out of the cell.

They found the armory in the guards' barracks, luckily in the half of the building not gutted by mortar shells. Outfitting the newly-freed prisoners with rifles and ammunition was the easy part. Most of the prisoners, while they looked a little rough from beatings, had managed to get themselves in fighting shape while in captivity, in part because there was nothing to do in prison except exercise, and also to build up muscle to withstand future beatings. The prisoners in worse shape than the first half would remain on the island, well-armed, until the rebels could send reinforcements and help them back to the mainland.

Finding food for those who had gone without for long periods was tougher, and the kitchen was quickly picked clean of portable items they could take along for the return trip home.

Stiletto only took a minute to greet the CIA agents he had come to rescue—Tim Pierce, and Johnny Powell. They said their third team mate, Townsend, had died after their recent beating. Lopez threw him in the ocean, Pierce said. They'd lost a fourth man in the ambush resulting in their capture. He'd been fed to the sharks, too. Pierce and Powell looked rough, but both were on their feet and ready to use the Kalashnikov rifles they had collected from dead Minas troopers.

Arencibia and Castillo led everybody to the opposite side of the island where the other boats were tethered, and they quickly stuffed each one as full or fuller than the vessels were designed for. They had to hurry. Reinforcements would not come by land. The patrol helicopters would come out in force, and if the helicopter gunners caught them on open water, they'd have very little ability to avoid the machine gun blasts.

The line of boats departed the island, separated by several feet. The mines had been deactivated earlier, so they weren't worried about sudden explosions. The sharks were no matter, either. Fiberglass hulls, even sprinkled with salt, didn't taste very good.

Stiletto rode with Arencibia, who steered the boat via the control arm attached to the rear motor. Scott was clutching a liberated AK-12, the now-familiar Kalashnikov, stoked with a full magazine and a pouch of spare magazines, tied around his waist. Unlike the rest of the prisoners, Stiletto hadn't been at the prison long enough to get a jumpsuit. Instead, he remained in what was left of his tuxedo, and it was thrashed. Truly a tragic sight. The cuffs of the pants had torn in several spots, and the pants and shirt were well soiled. He had no idea what had become of the jacket.

To replace the falling-apart dress shoes, Stiletto had found a pair of combat boots in the armory. Ones that actually fit and hadn't come off the body of a dead Minas trooper.

"What's the colonel have in mind?" He had to speak up over the noise of the rear motor and the splashing of the sea water assaulting them.

"The Lopez scout troops will be dealt with first, then

the assault on the capital begins. Every rebel cell has its list of targets. Strikes will be coordinated." Arencibia wiped a spray of water from his face.

Stiletto agreed with the plan. "Does the colonel know we have his son?"

"Not yet. I'll radio when we reach the shore."

Stiletto watched the mainland grow in size as the fleet neared. His stomach wasn't bothering him; a short boat ride he could handle. Longer? Not so much. But he had to hold on tight to a hand grip on the gunwale to keep his balance.

Stiletto looked at the front end of the boat, where Carlos Verduzco sat with the two surviving CIA agents.

Stiletto knelt in front of them. It was time for a formal introduction.

"Not much of a rescue, is it?"

"We're out," said Pierce. Then he frowned. "Are you Stiletto?"

"Yeah."

"The guy who got fired?"

"Why does everybody keep reminding me of that?"

"You're like a rock star to some of us," Pierce told him.

"My job is to get you two back to the United States, but I'm afraid our flight will be delayed until we help the rebels win a war. You two up for that?"

"You don't have to ask twice," said Johnny Powell.

Pierce said, "I should tell you about the arguments I

had with the brass at home about that very topic."

"Good."

Then Carlos Verduzco yelled, "Choppers!"

Two Huey gunships appeared over the tops of the trees ahead of them, the noses zeroing on the fleet of motorboats. Prisoners in some of the other boats started to fire, but Stiletto knew the salvos would be ineffectual at this point. It was better to wait until the helicopters were closer. The problem with that strategy was that it also meant the choppers would be close enough to fill every motorboat full of holes and drown every single person who rode in them, if the chopper pilots didn't first use their rocket pods to simply blast every boat out of the water.

Stiletto, Johnny Powell, and Tim Pierce hunkered down beside the gunwale, Carlos Verduzco easing next to Scott. Arencibia increased speed, the ride becoming bumpy, more spray blasting their faces.

"Why am I suddenly reminded of the Alamo?" Pierce asked.

CHAPTER FIFTEEN

The choppers opened with rockets.

Stiletto cursed the day those pilots were born.

The Mk40 FFAR 2.75-inch rockets on either side of the lead Huey were part of the UH-1's standard armament, which also included an M134 minigun and a swivel-mounted M-60. Knowing the capabilities of the choppers did not make facing them any easier. The left rocket pod of the lead Huey flashed smoke and fire and a string of six rockets headed for the fleet.

Arencibia opened the throttle, the boat lurching ahead, while others in the fleet sped up or tried to take evasive action. Two collided, but the rest spread out in a wide pattern, the rockets only impacting with the surface of the water. Just because they missed didn't mean the salvo hadn't scored. The explosions rocked the water, waves hitting Stiletto's boat and almost tipping it over. Scott shouted, "Let 'em have it!" and started firing his Kalashnikov in controlled bursts as the lead chopper flew overhead. He was rewarded with sparks on the underbelly, but that didn't mean they'd penetrated the chopper's steel skin.

Pierce, Powell, and Carlos Verduzco fired on the other chopper as it dipped to open fire, the second pilot choosing the mini-gun rather than rockets. He certainly had more ammo. The sudden buzz-saw effect of the weapon churning out six thousand rounds per minute of 7.62x51mm NATO was enough to chill the blood of anybody on the receiving end, and even Stiletto blanched as the rounds strafed the water between his boat and another, jets of spray flying skyward as the chopper passed. Everybody on the boat rotated their weapons to shoot the chopper, Scott aiming for the small tail rotor, cursing as his AK ran dry because there was no way he had hit the small moving target.

"Almost to shore!" the major shouted.

The choppers made their next pass, zooming up the backside of the fleet, the ex-prisoners shooting now, but the next flash from the primary Huey's rocket pod made a direct hit on one of the boats. The explosion shook the water and sent debris flying. The second chopper loosed more from the minigun, but a quick portside turn by the target boat evaded disaster, the minigun slugs once again only smashing into the ocean's surface.

Stiletto slammed a fresh mag into the AK and sighted on the lead chopper, firing and finally seeing the Plexiglas cockpit crack. The chopper veered away. Pierce and Powell fired on the other, the minigun spitting flame again, strafing the water beside the boat and striking the fiberglass hull on the starboard side. The holes were big enough to let the splashing water into the boat.

The choppers pulled away, flying one behind the other as they made a wide circle. They were allowing the boats to get to shore. Stiletto looked ahead. The beach looked like a sanctuary from a distance. Once everybody was on the sand and trying to make their way up the sand to the jungle, the M-60 machine guns on the Hueys would tear them apart one by one like an elephant sucking flies of a horse's back.

But it appeared the drivers of the other boats saw the same problem since several of them broke off from the fleet and headed farther up or down the shoreline, where they might find alternate means to get to the safety of the jungle. That was good and bad, but Stiletto wasn't in a position to hold a conference on the matter. They had to act now, and it seemed like the best course of action.

The chopper pilots saw what was happening too, and started flying to the easy targets, the ones closest to them, who were off to Stiletto's right. They had plenty of time, after all. Rockets flashed, and several explosions echoed. Stiletto kept his eyes forward. They were approaching the shore fast.

Arencibia shouted, "Hang on!"

Everybody grabbed hold of something as the bow of the boat sliced through the last of the water and dug into the sand, coming to a sudden halt that made everybody lurch forward. Pierce tumbled to the deck, and Powell helped him to his feet. Stiletto jumped out to provide cover while the others exited.

Two more boats pulled ashore at the same time, Sergeant Castillo and his team aboard one, ex-prisoners on another, and the beach filled with running men as they headed across the soft sand. The canopies of the trees above would protect them from the onslaught of the Huey gunships, but what about ground forces? Were troops on the way to join the fight? As Stiletto's boots sank into the sand and he ran awkwardly, he realized the helicopters weren't the only threat.

They were only the first wave.

And Stiletto, Arencibia, and the rest of the merry band of misfits were all running short of ammo, never mind the strength needed to run and fight.

Stiletto's lungs burned as he hustled, his boots sinking into the sand, the normal traction he'd have on paved ground nonexistent. He kept the Kalashnikov pointed ahead, knowing that if the ground troops arrived before they reached the jungle, they'd be sitting ducks between them and the helicopters. The helicopters were still busy at the other end of the beach. Stiletto didn't allow his thoughts to linger too long on the former prisoners who had taken that route, but he was grateful, and they gave the rest of them the chance to finish the war.

Finally, he reached the jungle and fell onto his side, trying to catch his breath. Others followed after, they too dropping as they succumbed to the need for a brief respite. Then Stiletto heard Carlos Verduzco call his name. He jumped back to his feet. Carlos had Pierce draped across his shoulders. He was bogged down in the sand. Scott raced to them, and they grabbed Pierce from either end, Carlos his shoulders, Stiletto his ankles. Walking backward, Stiletto helped get Pierce to cover. As they placed him on the ground, Pierce let out a yell.

"What happened?"

"Ran out of gas," Powell said, joining them.

Agony filled Pierce's face, but he managed to talk.

"I'll be fine," he said, wincing with the words.

More men moved past them, Arencibia eventually catching up and taking Powell's place on Pierce's left side. The CIA officer grabbed his midsection and rolled to his left, letting out a cry of pain.

Castillo ran over, removing his first aid kit and inspecting the CIA man. He told Pierce to move his hands and Pierce reluctantly did so, Castillo opening the jumpsuit so he could see what Pierce was grabbing at. The man's body was covered with dark welts, cuts, and bruises; there was no specific wound in the spot he'd grabbed. Castillo said, "Cramps."

"He ain't the only one," Stiletto said, groaning and bending slightly because of the cramping in his gut.

Arencibia stepped away to talk on his hand-held radio, and Stiletto watched him. Calling Colonel Verduzco, probably. When the major called Carlos over to talk to his father, Stiletto had no doubt.

The conversation didn't take long, and Stiletto heard very little, but it wasn't his business anyway. His cramps began to subside. By then, the radio conversation had concluded, and Arencibia approached the scattered group.

"We can't stay here," Major Arencibia stated. "Is this everybody?"

Stiletto quickly counted about fifteen gasping and prostrate men in their cluster.

Stiletto said, "Where's your mortar crew?"

"Two clicks that way," Arencibia said, pointing to his left. "Rally up and let's go!"

The scout team sent by the late Warden Lopez to check on the location of the rebel camp never saw the men who killed them.

Colonel Ciro Verduzco took the lead in the ambush squad, lining up his men about five kilometers outside the camp. The troops at the camp did not break down any-thing in preparation to leave since their orders were to make everything appear normal. There was some risk in that, in case any of the attackers survived the ambush, but the colonel had brought twenty troopers, all armed with heavy machine guns supplied by the Americans, and he didn't expect anybody to walk away from the onslaught of hot lead.

As the colonel waiting in the heavy undergrowth, his cap on tight, sweat trickling down his neck, he felt a surge of confidence and pride—everything he'd lacked since Carlos' capture. Hearing his son's voice, knowing he was free, had cleared the flog that had blocked his mind and crippled his leadership for so long. Now it was time to finish the fight. Now it was time to free his country.

Any moment now. . .

Finally, the scouting party appeared, moving parallel to the ambush line. They were much better at moving through the jungle than Verduzco would have given them credit for earlier. Guard duty on the prison island didn't give them much chance to practice such maneuvers, but they moved quietly, spread out with plenty of space between each man, their platoon leader the tip of their spear. They were almost within the kill zone of the ambush line.

Verduzco shouldered his American M-4 carbine. He'd already clicked off the safety catch. He was going to send a 5.56mm tumbler into that platoon leader's left ear, and his shot would be the signal for the rest of his men to open up with the machine guns. This fight would be over before it began.

A little bit more . . .

Verduzco eased back the trigger and let the M-4's recoil push against his shoulder.

The M-4 cracked, and the full-metal jacket slug closed

the distance between Verduzco and the platoon leader in the blink of an eye, the bullet plowing through the platoon leader's left ear as desired, the man's body dropping like a puppet with its strings cut. Any and all other sound was drowned out as the machine gunners opened fire, the jungle filling with the acrid scent of cordite and the shockwaves of muzzle blasts.

The unending salvo cut through the jungle, ripping through foliage, chopping through tree trunks, leveling not only the men in the kill zone but a portion of the jungle as well. When the shooting finally stopped, Verduzco rose like a phoenix from the flames.

Quickly he shouted orders for his men to rally and return to the camp.

Next, he'd send out the general alert to all rebel positions and tell them to gather at the main staging site, set up many months earlier, to go over final plans prior to attacking the capital and the presidential palace. Rebels units standing by in the capital city would get a separate message coordinating their efforts. The time for indecision had come to an end. It was time to end the terror of Lazaro Minas once and for all.

The gunfire from the choppers, and the choppers themselves, faded. They had no more targets to shoot. A few passes along the shore's edge, a few bursts to see if any rebels scurried, and that was the end.

Stiletto, Arencibia, and their crew marched carefully, slowly, since everybody needed time to recover, but there was no time to sit. Pierce was back on his feet, albeit a little unsteady at times, and Scott wondered if the man was injured worse than he realized. He was certainly hurt worse than he looked. What he needed, what they all needed, was rest and water, and Pierce needed a doctor. Scott had no idea how long it might be before they achieved that goal.

They linked up with the mortar crew, who already had their tubes disassembled and were waiting to move out. Having more guns on their side made Stiletto feel a little better, but they could still be overrun by any ground forces heading their way.

Though he had to admit, none had arrived yet. Were they truly on their way, or was he thinking paranoid?

It didn't make sense to send only the choppers.

At least they could make the most of the delay and continue the march back to the rebel camp.

"Not much farther," Arencibia said.

"To the camp?"

"To where we left our trucks."

"You didn't tell me you had trucks, major."

"You think we walked all the way here? We have trucks, there's a road, and everything is going to be okay."

Stiletto allowed himself a nervous chuckle and glanced behind him. The faces of the others, including the CIA men, seemed to lighten at the news. A truck sure beat marching through the jungle.

At least Tim Pierce was still on his feet, moving slowly, but still moving. He held his rifle like a man ready to use it, and he probably was.

Stiletto wondered what had happened to the former prisoners who had broken off from the line of boats. Had all of them been killed? Would they meet some on the way? Scott shook his head. As much as he was concerned about their fate, it was out of his hands. His job now was to keep the CIA men alive and help the rebels oust Minas from power. Staying for the final battle was outside his mission mandate, but what was Number One going to do, fire him? The old man knew Stiletto better than Scott knew himself, and remaining to aid the rebels would have been predicted, expected, and probably the reason Number One had called him to begin with.

The sight of the two trucks spurred everybody on, and they quickly leaped aboard, Sergeant Castillo jumping behind the wheel of the lead truck and twisting the ignition key. The engine rumbled to life. Some of the former prisoners jumped in the back of Castillo's truck, with Stiletto, Arencibia, the CIA men, and Carlos heading for the second. Arencibia drove. They pulled away from the roadside cutout and started along a paved roadway.

In the bed of the truck, Stiletto, the CIA men, and Carlos Verduzco shared the space, everybody sitting close and low so their heads didn't make obvious targets.

"We started out in a truck like this," Powell said.

Pierce managed a laugh. "We better not end in a truck like this."

Scott didn't have the energy to talk. Tim Pierce sat against the right side of the truck and groaned as the wheels went over bumps, but otherwise, all was quiet over the rumbling motor and exhaust.

Zurich

Harry Able was not a commando and didn't pretend to be a commando, but he had to join the four-man strike team making its way to Ramon Salazar's rented home.

The Big Guy, Number One, had finally made the decision after another meeting with Harry and Melissa Jarrett to grab Salazar and make him talk. Taking custody of Jenny Farnsworth had proved uneventful. She'd willingly surrendered and was once again telling her story to the security people at The Trust's nerve center.

She knew nothing about Salazar's home. She'd never been there. She had no idea if the domicile was booby-trapped, or if Salazar had access to firearms. The four-man strike team was, of course, prepared to deal with such matters. They were dressed head-to-toe in black combat gear, wearing body armor, and carrying the latest in submachine guns.

Harry Able, in his suit and tie, felt very much out of place.

But he felt very much like he needed to be there to see his investigation through to the end.

They traveled in a blacked-out van along Witkoner-strasse through a quiet neighborhood of homes and small shops and restaurants. Harry hated the idea of disturbing the peace at so late an hour. It was well after 2 a.m., but the tactical commander had said it was always best to hit a target when he was asleep. Assuming Ramon Salazar kept normal hours, of course. The security team that had tracked Salazar confirmed he had a normal bedtime of midnight, but that didn't mean the Venezuelan operative couldn't throw a monkey wrench into his usual routine.

Harry should have been in bed too. He was fortified with several cups of coffee and expected adrenaline to provide the boost required to get through the raid. Luck-ily, he'd get to stay in the van and observe. He wasn't sure he could keep up with the strike team. They were all much fitter than he. Harry needed to hit the gym and hit it hard. Too many years behind a desk were showing in ways he hadn't realized when he compared himself to the door-kickers on the strike team.

The van slowed and made a turn. The strike team be-gan communicating in verbal shorthand as they made a final check of their gear and communications.

Salazar's house sat the corner of Witkonerstrasse and Berghaldenstrasse, with a park next door on the left side, more homes on the right, and other homes across the street. They had determined that approaching the rear of Salazar's home via the park made the most sense. Hit from behind, and any shooting on Salazar's part would end up in the open field behind his house. The strike team would have to make sure their bullets didn't go beyond Salazar's front door and across the street, but Harry knew they could control that better than allowing Salazar to potentially spray automatic weapons fire in the direction of innocent people.

The van pulled over near the park. The strike team commander threw open the sliding door on the passenger side and he and his three men exited quickly, melting into the early morning shadows of the park. Harry left his rear seat and pulled the sliding door shut. He remained with one person, a woman named Amanda, as she sat in front of monitors and a computer terminal. Cameras on the roof of the van displayed images of the park and Salazar home on the monitors. She spoke into a headset as she communicated with the team about the state of the home. Lights out, no sign of movement. Harry took a seat close to Amanda, but not so close that she'd notice. Her eyes were focused on the monitors and her workstation. Harry took a deep breath. He felt nervous, and his hands were shaking. He could only imagine what the strike team felt while he was safe in the van. He felt bad for feeling nervous.

The glow of the monitors filled the van's interior, bothering Harry's eyes. He didn't understand how Amanda could stare at them without reducing the brightness.

Sudden chatter on the radio made Harry's stomach tighten. They were going in!

Strike team commander said, "In position, back of the house. Everybody copy?"

Each member of the strike force signaled their readiness.

"We're moving in."

Amanda said, "Copy, I see you."

Harry moved closer to her. The silhouettes of the strike team appeared on the monitor, spaced out at pre-determined intervals, two stopping while two others moved forward to the back patio doors. The doors, the sliding glass variety, revealed nothing of the darkened interior of the house.

Their communications were on a scrambled frequency to prevent the local cops from picking up the transmission. That was the one aspect Harry didn't like. He would have wanted to alert the Zurich police to what was happening, perhaps enlist their assistance, but Number One had nixed the idea. If all went well, they could be in and out with Salazar in custody before the police even received a notification about the incident. But Harry was well aware that everybody had the perfect plan until the other side threw the first punch.

"Breaching now," the team commander said.

Harry Able caught himself holding his breath and sucked in a lungful of air. He forced himself to keep breathing.

The two strike team operatives approaching the patio

doors placed their explosives and moved to the side, and the resulting blast shattered the windows and created a spill of glass on the patio. The other two strike team members rushed inside, the last two following, the monitors still showing a dark interior but with the bouncing beams of lights mounted on the forward stock of the teams' submachine guns.

"Contact!"

Automatic weapons fire crackled. To Harry, the shots sounded as if they were echoing throughout the neighborhood. The gunfire intensified for a moment, then ceased.

"Target down! We have target down!"

"Copy, target down," Amanda said. She began typing on her keyboard, sending a message back to Trust HQ, where Melissa Jarrett and Number One waited for news. She paused, and when a message came back to her, she said into her headset: "Collect all available material."

"In progress," replied the team commander.

Harry Able's shoulders slumped. Salazar dead? Would the team collect enough intelligence for them to sort out who his source at the CIA was, or were they up a creek without a paddle?

After two minutes, Amanda announced that police were on their way. The strike team hustled back to the van and the driver pulled away quietly, without screeching a tire. Harry stayed in the back, out of sight, as the team settled in with the information they had gathered, mostly papers, a computer, other items. He'd never felt so useless in his life. The only thing to do now was get the material back to HQ and spend the rest of the night sorting.

Good thing he'd drunk all that coffee.

Minas ordered General Vitorio Florez to increase security at his home.

"That may mean," the general said, "pulling troops from other areas. Vital areas."

"Are you arguing with me, General Florez?"

They stood in the walkway outside the palace conference room, Minas dressed smartly in a tan suit, the general in his pressed military uniform.

"I am not arguing, but if what we see happening is true—"

"I have guests in the conference room," Minas said, stepping closer to Florez. The two nearly matched each other in height. "If something is happening, they need to be protected."

"Yes, Presidente. I will order additional troops here at once."

"Any word from Lopez?"

"We hear he is dead, Presidente."

"Are you sure? Positive?"

"It appears the prisoners are very much in charge of the prison. They are armed and patrolling the area."

Minas took a deep breath. He wanted to swallow the lump in his throat, but not with the general staring at him.

News of the prison raid meant only one thing: Verduzco had tossed out their gentleman's agreement about ceasing hostilities while the Verduzco son was at the prison, and now the rebels were mounting a full-on assault to depose him.

Because of the Americans.

It was always their fault.

And he'd had no word from Salazar in Zurich for several hours. Was something happening there too?

It was the worst possible moment for such a development, since the "guests" in the conference room were the various members of the criminal elite making investments in Venezuela, for safe haven, and other incidentals.

"Don't stand here staring, General," Minas said. "I want those troops here immediately, and we must make plans to evacuate my guests to safety. Understand?"

"It will be done, Presidente."

Minas turned on his heel and marched back into the conference room. He did not pause to compose himself. This was not the time for lies. The time had come to be at least a little truthful because the situation on the streets in the capital city and elsewhere would make lying impossible.

Minas felt confident his military could crush the rebellion once the fighting began, but there was a part of him that knew desperate fighters couldn't be easily beaten. They would fight to the last man.

Or the last breath.

CHAPTER SIXTEEN

Stiletto and his convoy did not face any further assault by Minas' troopers.

They'd been fortunate, he knew. The two CIA men called it luck, but Stiletto didn't believe in luck. Only skill and focus would get them through this challenge and onto the next.

The two trucks turned off the paved road and into the dirt driveway of a small church. Stiletto asked Arencibia what they were doing.

"Church doubles as a hospital," the major explained.

Stiletto said okay. He received questioning looks from the CIA men and other prisoners, but Stiletto said nothing.

The church sat in the middle of an open area, what looked like a school building and playground on one side, a small cemetery on the other. There were rebel troops scattered about. Stiletto quickly determined that this was a rebel outpost and there happened to be a church there, too.

Those in the worst shape needed to stay at the church, the major said once he'd exited his truck. That included CIA man Tim Pierce and two others, who were visibly not in any condition to continue with the mission. Pierce didn't argue. He handed his partner, Johnny Powell, his automatic rifle, and introduced himself to the priest in charge of the church.

The padre's name was Dominick; he was white and said he hailed from Brooklyn. He'd been stationed throughout Central America for two decades, and he and Stiletto chatted for a moment. Father Dom asked if he was one of the Americans who had brought their medical supplies. Stiletto admitted he was. Father Dom told him they had a good chance of nursing the wounded back to health because of that medicine; Stiletto had done them a world of good. Stiletto said, "I wasn't alone. I had help."

"You have a lot of help," Father Dom said. "That help will stay with you on the next part of your journey."

"How are you and the nuns fixed for defenses?"

Father Dom laughed. "We have a small squad of rebels here. The government leaves us alone because attacking a church is bad news no matter how it's spun. And if all else fails, I have this." The padre opened his robe enough to show Stiletto the gleaming stainless-steel revolver on his hip.

"A cowboy priest, huh?"

Father Dom smiled. "I grew up in Brooklyn, remember?"

One of the nuns, a woman maybe five feet tall, jogged

over. She said something to the priest, who turned to Stiletto.

"The man Pierce would like to see you. Sister Ruth will show you."

Stiletto followed the nun into the church, where the bare essentials were standard. The well-worn pews had seen better days. The walls were painted white, with various busts and paintings on either side.

But that was not where Sister Ruth took Stiletto. They continued to the front of the church and around the back of the cross, to a set of steps leading to the basement. Down below was a full hospital, brightly lit and well-stocked with medical equipment and nuns in full nurse mode. The beds were full, the American CIA man and several of the prisoners at the end of a row. The rest of the beds contained men and women Stiletto did not know personally, but he recognized soldiers when he saw them. Some looked healed and ready to leave; others, not so much.

Stiletto stopped by Pierce. A nun was in the process of hooking up an IV. She kept her eyes on her work as the men talked.

"Better than Johns Hopkins," Pierce said. He forced a laugh. The nun inserted the IV line into a vein on his left arm, and he winced.

"You're gonna be fine," Stiletto said. "Take it easy and do what they tell you."

"Hey, how 'bout a favor?"

"What?"

"I got a kid. She lives in Idaho. Twin Falls. If anything happens to me, you know—"

Stiletto froze. He knew all too well what Tim Pierce was asking, and there was no way he could say no.

"I'll do whatever you ask, Tim."

Tim Pierce opened a pocket of his prison jumpsuit. "I kept this from the prison guards," he said, handing Stiletto a folded photograph. Stiletto took the picture. "Her name is Shelly."

The photo showed a pretty blonde woman in her 20s. She had green eyes, and a smile that, Stiletto assumed, resembled her mother's, but she had her father's nose. Fathers and daughters were connected like that.

"Tell her, you know, her old man—"

"I get it. I have a daughter too."

"Yeah."

The two men said nothing for a moment.

"You better get going. Win the war, rock star."

"Hold onto this for me," Stiletto said, handing back the girl's picture. "I don't think I'm going to need it."

Pierce smiled. Stiletto shook his hand, the CIA man's grip weaker than the last time they'd shaken, and nodded his thanks to the nun. He made his way back to the ground floor.

The trucks' engines were rumbling, Arencibia waving at Stiletto to hurry. He ran to the truck, where Father Dom waited.

Father Dom said, "God bless you."

"I'll be back, padre."

"I know."

Stiletto hopped into the truck bed and slapped the roof of the cab.

The two trucks drove away from the church. Stiletto didn't look back.

Men with guns surrounded them.

There were some women in the mix, too. And teen-agers, Stiletto noted. All ready for a fight. All looking at the arriving trucks like hungry sharks. When Arencibia and Castillo leaned out the driver's side windows of the trucks, they calmed down. When Arencibia began shouting that they had rescued the colonel's son, they cheered.

Stiletto jumped down from the back of the truck and was immediately swept aside by the crowd rushing Carlos Verduzco. He wore a wide-open grin as he was greeted by his fellow warriors, and was almost carried from the truck to where his father waited. When father and son finally embraced, Stiletto felt a glow of accomplishment. One goal achieved. Now the bigger obstacle remained.

Arencibia had not told Stiletto much about the gathering point from which the assault on the capital city would originate, but as Stiletto looked around, he noted the flat area surrounded by trees, with a rock formation in the center forming a sort of stage, wide across the top and planted firmly in the dirt.

The colonel stepped up onto the rock with his son in tow, holding his son's left arm up, proclaiming the rescue a great victory. Once the crowd finally calmed down, Verduzco began a pep talk to get the soldiers ready for the attack. Stiletto didn't think they needed one. They were primed and ready to go without any further ado.

"Hey."

Stiletto turned. Beth Carrington smiled at him.

"Been wondering when you'd catch up."

"It's been a rough day," he told her.

"Feel like getting out of what's left of that tux?"

He frowned.

"Idiot. Here." She shoved his pack into his gut. Hard. "Change of clothes. Your pistol is there too."

"Bless your heart, Beth."

"I'm afraid the scotch didn't survive."

Stiletto sniffed the pack. "I can tell. Wow. What did that scotch ever do to anybody?"

"Check your cigars, too."

"I'm sure they're fine." Stiletto grinned and separated from the rally, finding a spot behind a cluster of trees to change. The uniform fit well. It felt great to strap on his shoulder harness with the Colt Combat Government tucked inside and two spare magazines under his right arm. He was ready for a real fight once again. Checking the pack further, he found the beef stick and cheese were gone. The scotch he knew about, the pack still wet from where the bottle broke, and when he pulled out the plastic container holding his cigars, he noted no damage on the outside, which meant the stickers inside were probably all right. He opened it quickly to make sure; all cigars intact. After what he'd been through, he needed a puff. Selecting a La Galera corona, Stiletto lit the cigar and sat back against the tree trunk with a relaxing exhale.

He listened absently to Verduzco's pep talk. It was the kind of speech that had been delivered by officers to soldiers throughout history, punctuated by cheers from the fighters.

"May I join you?"

Stiletto scooted aside to make room for Beth. She draped her automatic rifle across her lap.

"He's not talking to us," she said.

"No, but he could be."

"Did you find the CIA agents?"

"Two dead, one at a church hospital, the other's around here somewhere getting kitted out, I assume." He explained about leaving Tim Pierce behind. He did not tell her about his request.

"Are you storming the capital?" she said.

"You're welcome to stay behind. I have to go."

"Have to, or want to?"

"Both."

"You're a complex man, Scott. I thought I had you figured out in the beginning."

Stiletto absently dug into the dirt with the heel of his left boot. He didn't look at Beth. "What do you think now?"

"I don't know what to think, but you're a good man to have in a fight."

"So are you. Does that mean I was right?"

"That'd we'd be friends by the time this mission was over?"

"I thought I said something like that, yeah."

She smiled. "I suppose I'll add you to my Facebook, sure."

"Everybody knows that doesn't mean anything."

"It's all you're going to get right now."

"You New Hampshire girls like to play cards close to your chest, don't you?"

"Is that what we're known for?"

"That and having families with more money than my father has made in his lifetime."

"It's not all like that," Beth argued.

"Are we going to help free Venezuela and have another story we can never tell anybody?"

"At this point, I don't think I could refuse."

Stiletto blew out smoke. "Don't get killed."

"You either."

Stiletto smiled.

"You're coming with us."

Stiletto raised an eyebrow at Colonel Verduzco and his son. The rally was over, and the troops were on their way. Trucks rumbled as they started off from the gathering point and headed for their attack's staging points. Exhaust fumes were pungent.

"You and Miss Carrington," the colonel continued, "and the CIA man, Powell."

"Are you sure you want Americans at the palace?" he said.

"At this point, it doesn't matter. If you get killed, we'll figure out a solution."

"I want a crack at Minas as much as you do, Colonel."

"May the best man take his head off," the colonel said, offering his hand. Stiletto laughed, and they shook heartily.

"Where's the major going?" Stiletto said as Arencibia loaded his crew onto a truck and prepared to move out.

"Television station," Verduzco said. "They'll seize that and begin broadcasting the message that the coup has begun. Our people in the other cities will take on any troops they find, and hopefully keep the army from converging on us at the capital."

"Will anybody in the army switch sides?"

"We're counting on it, but we have no idea how many might," Verduzco said.

"We're facing incredible odds with no promise of success," Stiletto continued.

"Minas is too."

"Do we have any idea how many troops are guarding the palace?"

Verduzco shrugged. "All of them, probably."

"Then it sounds like we're about even, Colonel. When do we leave?"

If any of the "guests" noticed the arrival of troops via large transport vehicle, none of them said anything to El Presidente Minas.

If any of the guests noticed Minas sweating under his shirt despite the ceiling fans circulating the air from outside the conference room, they didn't let on.

All Minas knew was that he was spinning his wheels, talking business, trying to convince himself more than the others that everything was normal.

Everything was not normal.

He stood in front of the table, as usual, those seated the members of the crime community who had agreed to invest in Venezuelan infrastructure in return for a cut of the profits, and, of course, their own safe haven within the country should such safe haven be required. Among the French and Italian gangsters and drug dealers, the American Mafia, and other assorted misfits, sat the luscious Nikki Fortune, who followed Minas' movements with her big, dark eyes. She had previously not wanted to include herself among the nation's investors, but, apparently, her father wanted more information, and was willing to throw money into the pot if the deal sounded right. Minas allowed her to sit in and listen.

The rebels had rescued the Verduzco kid, and now

Minas was marked for death unless his army stopped the assault on the capital in general and the palace in particular.

Should the worst happen, Minas had an evacuation plan for his guests, although he'd planned to use the route for himself. And maybe Clarissa, too. Probably.

Eventually, one of the two Frenchman around the table, who was in charge of a France-Italy drug corridor, asked why all the troops were arriving.

"Precautionary measures, I'm afraid," Minas said. "There are rumors of an uprising about to happen."

That received more attention than anything else Minas had said in the last half hour.

"Whoa!" one of the Americans said. "You mean you're being attacked?"

"Trouble in the cities," Minas replied. "We are safe here."

"Yeah, but what if we aren't?" the American asked. Others grumbled in agreement.

"If the worst happens, we proceed to the basement. When this palace was built, I constructed an underground tunnel network that will take us to safety."

The Fortune woman laughed. Minas locked eyes with her as a hot flush crawled the length of his neck. He didn't appreciate others laughing at him. Especially women.

"We are safe, I promise," Minas said.

And then the first bombs struck. The building shook.

CHAPTER SEVENTEEN

Stiletto had traded his AK-12 for a US M-4 carbine to match what the rest of the strike team carried, and his upper body felt the weight of the extra mags stuffed into his chest rig. Beth and Powell were similarly armed, although Stiletto was the only one with a handgun for backup. The Colt Combat Government pistol rode under his left arm.

Scott, Beth Carrington, and CIA contractor Johnny Powell marched uphill alongside Colonel Verduzco and his hand-picked team of fighters, which included his son, Carlos. Their job was to attack Minas' palace from behind, the point of the V, because that was where the man's conference room, bedroom, and office were located and where he spent most of his time. The remaining force would attack head-on; mortars first, then blow a hole in the wall surrounding the estate and rush in like so many bees escaping a hive.

The colonel signaled a halt, and the strike force dropped prone at the base of the estate's rear wall. Beyond, Stiletto knew from his visit during the birthday party for Mrs. Minas, lay the expansive back patio with its maze, statues, the pool, and, ultimately, the building.

Their goal was to get to Minas before he escaped during the first phase of the assault.

Stiletto kept his eyes ahead, scanning left and right. One thing Minas didn't have was a roving patrol. They'd encountered no troops during their climb. One on El Presidente's many mistakes.

It was a good day for a battle. The sky was clear, the humidity tolerable, and there was no wind. Stiletto almost felt bad for disturbing Mother Nature's peace with more violence and death, but Minas had rung up a high butcher's bill, and it needed to be paid. With his blood.

Nobody spoke. They were waiting for the bombs to drop.

Then then the explosions started.

The mortar crew was positioned to the northeast of the estate, hiding in a small open area of the surrounding forest that had a perfect line-of-sight to the palace grounds. As the bombs hit, a loud klaxon started wailing, the sound carrying well beyond the estate's grounds. Another blast, and the crackles of automatic weapons fire began. That was when Verduzco and another trooper planted a block of C-4 at the base of the rear wall, set a timer, and ordered everybody to get to cover.

The C-4 detonated and blew chunks of concrete in every direction, but the worst were the tiny particles that whipped past and tore into exposed skin if said particles found spots to land. The bigger chunks landed on the ground and started to roll downhill. Colonel Verduzco sounded the battle cry of, "Go forward!" and the strike team rushed through the gap in the wall and onto the rear of the grounds.

Stiletto had told the crew to avoid going to the right since that would put them in line with the swimming pool, and that wasn't an easy obstacle to navigate around. The team stayed to the left, racing up the line of hedgerows, dodging the marble statues, getting closer to the building.

When troopers with red X patches on their shoulders responded to the back-wall breach blast, their Kalashnikov rifles spit flame. The strike team spread out… and immediately encountered the first problem with the hedgerows. Anybody hiding behind them lost visual contact with whatever was in front of them.

A burst of AK fire split the top of the hedgerow Stiletto and Beth lay behind as Scott was trying to find a gap to see through. Other strike team members fired back, the rebel soldiers calling out to each other as they fired and moved, and Stiletto whistled for Johnny Powell, who had found a hiding spot behind a statue. Powell fired a covering burst, then scooted from that position to where Scott and Beth waited.

"I said to not go near the pool, right?" Stiletto asked.

"Right," said Powell.

"I think we can flank the enemy if we go that way, but

be careful not to fall in. You're gonna get caught in the open, too, if they see us there."

"We need to move," Beth added.

Spoken like a combat vet. Stiletto said, "Follow me" and scooted past Powell to move to the right of the strike force, the enemy fire not reaching them as they crawled along the length of the hedge. But then the hedge ended. The concrete surrounding the pool opened up wide, the pool taking up most of the space.

"Three- to five-second rushes," Stiletto said. "Stay close to the hedges."

Beth and Powell acknowledged.

The sounds of the battle up front grew more intense, the deafening noise and tunnel vision beginning to effect Stiletto's senses. He again took the lead, leaving the cover of the hedge to run forward, counting down in his head. He fired at the Minas troopers who were weaving through the hedges to engage the rebel forces head-on. Stiletto's bursts didn't connect, but they'd for sure feel the fire coming from a different direction, and the psychological effect of believing they were caught in a crossfire would make more than one of Minas' soldiers hesitate before he made another move.

Four seconds. Stiletto dropped and rolled behind a hedge maybe twenty meters from the house.

Directly left, down the row between his hedge and the one behind him, he had a different view of the enemy. They were still focused on the colonel and his team. Stiletto changed magazines in the M-4 and let off a string of single shots, dropping one of the Minas soldiers and driving the others to cover once more. He pivoted right, facing the building, firing wildly, but no troopers were coming from that direction. He dropped again as Beth joined him.

Scott and Beth fired to provide Powell cover, and as the CIA contractor reached them, he tripped and crashed headlong into the hedge. Working his way out, he brushed debris off his chest and face and stifled a laugh.

"The audience wants an encore," Stiletto told him. "And I want to get into that building."

Johnny Powell remarked, "It looks like a Motel 6."

"We used that joke already," Stiletto said.

"I'll cover you," the CIA man said. He fired over the hedge and Stiletto bolted. Three seconds this time. Down again, rolling left. Beyond the pool now, maybe fifteen meters away. The right side of the V was clearly visible now, both levels clear of activity. If anybody was inside, they were hunkered down. Or they were fighting up front. A glance toward the wide expanse of grass and palm trees farther ahead showed a furious battle, smoke drifting across the grass, non-stop gunfire, and palm trees struck down by the falling mortars.

The scent of smoke and cordite was almost overpowering.

Beth landed beside Scott, and Powell joined her a moment after.

"Mad dash to the wall," Stiletto said.

"Go!" Powell barked. He fired another covering burst. Stiletto took off. Beth kept up beside him, leaving enough space in case they needed to drop and roll. Powell picked up the rear. Their boots hit the concrete of the outer walkway on the first floor. They slammed their backs to the wall, looking back and forth.

"Where's the elevator?" Powell asked.

"Stairwell," Stiletto replied. "It's a motel, remember?"

"Lead the way," Beth said. A layer of sweat covered her face, but her eyes were open and alert, ready for anything.

"To the right."

Stiletto started forward, moving at a quick clip and staying close to the wall. They were heading for the point of the V, and hopefully Lazaro Minas himself.

It was like a game of Whack-a-Mole.

Except if you got whacked, you might not get up again.

Colonel Ciro Verduzco felt red-hot hate in his veins as he popped up over the top of a hedge, letting his M-4 do the talking. He stroked the trigger, the muzzle spitting flame, the shoulder stock kicking into his shoulder. He fired a short burst, shifted his aim, and fired another. A Minas trooper went down. Verduzco dropped and rolled left as return fire split the air where he'd been, cutting into the hedge and ricocheting off the concrete pathway. One of the ricochets buzzed past his back.

He lifted his head enough to see Stiletto, Beth Carrington, and Johnny Powell making a run for the building. He plucked a grenade from his belt. He and Stiletto had talked about the line of people waiting to kill Minas, and the American had found a way to cut in line. Verduzco pulled the pin on the grenade and lobbed it toward the enemy. He shouted, "Grenade!" prior to the detonation, which shook the ground beneath him. Up again, with his M-4 spitting lead. He ceased fire. There were no more enemies to shoot.

His son Carlos took a knee beside him. "The Americans—"

"Running for the building. We have to cover them."

Verduzco stood up and shouted for his men to follow him. The rebel troops ran the zigzag of hedgerows, some ignoring the hedges and pushing through gaps created by the grenade blast. They didn't give one thought to the shattered bodies of the Minas soldiers as they hurried over them. The men had deserved worse than the quick exit of a grenade blast.

Verduzco and his son headed for the house. The battle out front intensified with the blasts of heavy artillery. Verduzco wasn't concerned. The big guns represented two rebel tanks that had made their way up the access road to the house. The Minas troops didn't have tanks. The battle at the palace would end soon, although Colonel Verduzco knew that still meant one way or another. Now was not the time to take anything for granted.

"Where do you want the bomb, Major?"

"Drop it on the front porch."

"Yes, sir."

The mortar man placed a high-explosive shell on the lip of the mouth of the mortar tube, then let it fall the length of the steel container, and he and Major Arencibia turned their backs and covered their necks.

The tube belched.

Seconds later, the front door of the capital city's television station vaporized in a flash of fire, and the major and the mortar man feeling the wave from the concussion that followed.

The television station in the business park was the prize for Arencibia and his crew after they defeated the token resistance. Minas had not left a sizeable force at the station, one of many in the country, but the main broadcasting source in the capital. Arencibia and his team, riding in on armored transport vehicles complete with heavy machine guns, made mincemeat of the troopers outside. Those left inside, the station employees and their government-supplied overlords, would have the option to surrender, but if they picked up weapons from the fallen, Arencibia's men had orders to terminate with extreme prejudice.

The major's assault on the television station was made

easier by the embedded rebel fighters already in the capital who, on the colonel's radio signals, began their offensive. They started with coordinated bombings at police stations and engagements with troops on the street. Various parts of the capital were on fire, long columns of smoke trailing skyward, the pops of automatic gunfire echoing on a continuous loop.

"One more," Arencibia told the mortar man. "Knock out the front windows."

The young mortar man adjusted the aiming unit on the launch tube and dropped a shell, and they turned around. The next explosion sent a barrage of steel and glass onto the street, the smoke thick. The major then called for the main assault. His troops swarmed across the street, converging on the building as station employees, dirtied and coughing, marched out with a white flag. One group of rebels separated the employees and took them aside. The rest of the force entered the building. The station employees warned of armed government people inside, but before the rebels could radio the information, gunshots sounded. It was only a brief barrage. Rebel troops inside radioed that the major could now enter the building.

Arencibia left the mortar position and ran across the street, ignoring the bluster of the station employees, who demanded to know what was going on. Arencibia moved through the cluster of cubicles and open desks inside the building, crossing the room to a control center secured by his men. Arencibia didn't pretend to understand what the monitors and electronic panels did, but two of his people knew. He ignored the dead government people on the floor, most clutching pistols in their now dead hands.

As two of his men worked the consoles, Arencibia removed from inside his BDU blouse a flash drive. He passed it to one of his men, who plugged it into the main broadcast feed after killing the broadcast of a soap opera. Soon Colonel Verduzco's face filled the monitors as he announced the coup in progress and that El Presidente Minas would soon be removed and freedom and justice restored to Venezuela.

Arencibia allowed himself to take a short break as he watched the video. All they'd worked for was summed up on that monitor screen, and it felt good to finally see. He then started moving again, telling his squad commanders to form a perimeter around the building. The Verduzco broadcast would play in a loop so the entire country could see, but they had to keep the television station secured in case any government forces tried to retake it and kill the broadcast.

As he left the building, the major wondered how Verduzco and the Americans were doing at the presidential palace.

Because if the teams didn't succeed there, taking over the television station meant nothing.

Stiletto heard the grenade blast and the cessation of small-arms fire in the rear patio.

Most of the action was still at the front of the palace.

But Scott, Beth, and Johnny Powell ignored that as they moved along the wall, Powell covering their backsides, Beth watching the second-floor rail. Stiletto charged ahead. They stopped at a gap in the wall. Stiletto stepped away, his M-4 tucked into his shoulder, and began the slow process of moving in a semi-circle to get a look around the corner without sticking his head into view.

There was a set of concrete steps ahead, their black metal railing like so many other stairwells he'd seen. So much so that he felt an odd sense of familiarity. He kicked the thoughts out of his mind. There was nothing familiar up those steps, only his death if he remained distracted by Minas' architectural choices.

"Going up," Stiletto said.

He started forward, taking the steps cautiously and keeping the M-4 trained upward. There was only one landing ahead, and then the next flight of steps to the second floor.

He took one step, then paused.

Voices above. Panic. He tightened his grip on the M-4 and used his free hand to signal Beth and Powell to stop and drop.

The swaying chandelier above the conference table might as well have had a blade attached because Minas felt that at any second, he'd be cut in half.

"I need you all to remain calm and follow me outside," he said.

"Outside?" yelled one of the gangsters. Minas didn't bother to look at the faces any longer. "They're fighting outside!"

"It's the only way to get you out of here safely. Follow me."

Minas turned and headed for the door. He'd never expected to need the escape tunnels, and now he was running down the number of ways in which his construction of the palace had made such an escape more complicated, now that an armed force was in the middle of an attack.

He wanted to stop and see to his wife, Clarissa, but his guests took priority. The money they'd pour into his coffers took priority. Clarissa was a tough lady. She'd know what to do, and he had weapons stashed all over the place.

He led the group to the outside walkway. The main battle was happening in front and behind; General Florez would be up front, leading the defense force against the rebels. He had no worries. Failure was not in the general's vocabulary. The rebel attack had minutes, maybe less, before it ended and Minas' forces emerged victorious.

But he had to make sure the money was safe.

Drifting smoke stung eyes and forced coughs as the centipede of confused souls followed the leader of Venezuela, heading for a gap in the wall that signaled a stairwell.

As Minas hurried, he wished everybody behind him

would shut up. They were making far too much noise.

Minas had made one big mistake leaving the conference room, but he didn't know it. Had he looked at the faces behind him, he might have noticed.

Somebody had stayed behind.

Nikki Fortune peeked up from under the conference table.

Nobody had seen her duck below it during the rush to escape, and that hadn't surprised her. Crooks had more ego than sense; they only thought about themselves.

She knew because she was no different, despite contrary evidence which she refused to believe.

She eyed the connecting door as the building shook from the explosions outside. If Minas wanted to pull his Keystone Cop act with the big money, having grown such a huge head over his supposed God-like invincibility, let him. She wanted to see what she could find that might help Stiletto and the rebels after the fight.

She realized she hadn't been of much help other than to pass information to the late Warden Lopez, and her attempts to find out what had happened to Scott after the party had been overtaken by events.

But maybe she could still contribute something.

The connecting door opened as she twisted the knob. It hadn't been locked. The opulent bedroom beyond surprised her.

"It's about time you—" a woman began, but the words

cut off as quickly as she'd spoken them, replaced by, "That son of a bitch!"

Nikki Fortune let her mouth hang open at the sight before her.

The woman was obviously Mrs. Clarissa Minas, the lady of the house, whom Nikki had seen at the birthday party. She had dressed in jeans, boots, and a white blouse, put on a jacket, and packed a bag, which she held in her left hand. Totally casual. Never mind that bullets were flying and bombs were dropping. She'd taken the time to put on a posh escape outfit, and damn anybody who stood in her way. She'd been expecting her devoted husband to come through the door, only for that not to happen. The red flush now crawling up her neck told Nikki she'd have a fireball on her hands in nothing flat.

"He left without me?" the woman shouted, throwing her bag on the carpet.

For the first time in her life, Nikki was almost speechless. She managed, "Well—"

But Clarissa Minas wasn't finished.

"I'll bury that bastard myself! He knows I know everything! I know where his camps are, where he's keeping the special prisoners, I know what he's doing with all the money, I know it all!"

"We can wait here for the rebels," Nikki said. "I'll make sure nothing happens to you."

"Who the hell are you?"

"Nikki Fortune."

"What does that mean to me?"

"It means to you that the Americans know who I am, and they aren't going to kill me. They will also not kill anybody I tell them not to kill. Get it, sweetie?"

Clarissa Minas softened a little. She shrugged.

"Want a glass of wine?"

Stiletto gestured for Beth and Powell to move back off the steps. They complied, taking cover along the wall once again. Stiletto left the steps too, ducking around the corner opposite Beth and Powell and licking his lips in anticipation.

Footsteps clicked behind him. Stiletto swung around but froze as he identified Verduzco, father and son.

"Can't let you have all the fun," the colonel said.

Stiletto put a finger to his lips. The colonel nodded.

The line of men crowding down the steps finally cleared the stairway, Minas saying, "Stay behind me!" as he started onto the grass and a concrete square with a manhole cover in the center of the field.

Stiletto, the Verduzco pair, Beth, and Powell stepped out with their weapons up.

"Halt!" Stiletto shouted. The gangsters looking for an easy payday put their hands in the air and shouted jumbled words, while Minas let out a yell and ran for the manhole. The Verduzco pair ran after him, Carlos the younger diving for the man's legs. He wrapped both arms around

Minas' knees, and El Presidente fell like a chopped tree, hitting the ground face-first. Carlos jumped up as Minas tried to rise and clubbed him behind the head with the butt of his M-4. Minas dropped, but remained woozy, trying to lift his head.

Verduzco the elder rolled El Presidente onto his back. Minas looked up at them with woozy eyes, his mouth spouting nonsensical protests as the colonel waved Stiletto over.

Scott stopped beside the colonel. Minas had stopped talking and cast his glassy look across all three of their faces.

Behind them, Beth and Powell had the gangsters secured, herding them into the stairwell, where they forced them all to their knees at the points of their rifles.

Colonel Verduzco said, "A three-man firing squad is better than two."

"I concur," Stiletto agreed. "Shall we assume the position?"

Minas found his resolve as the three men put some space between each other, forming a semi-circle around the prostrate dictator.

"No! Don't do this! Don't kill me!"

Carlos Verduzco laughed. His father said nothing.

Minas turned his pleading eyes to Stiletto.

"Make them stop!"

Stiletto instead shouldered his M-4. The Verduzcos followed his example. The colonel counted down from three. Minas screamed. The rifles spit flame. Minas' body jerked as the lead bullets broke through the layers of clothing into his thick skin, splitting open flesh. Carlos Verduzco fired a last bullet through the middle of El Presidente's head. Minas' eyes remained open as he lay sprawled on the field of grass like a dead cow.

Stiletto and the Verduzcos lowered their weapons.

And, as if a switch had been flipped, the battle began to subside.

CHAPTER EIGHTEEN

"Hi, Scott," Nikki Fortune said. "Want a glass of wine?"

Stiletto frowned as he entered the Minas' bedroom from the outer walkway door. Nikki and Clarissa Minas sat on a couch, sipping from crystal glasses, seemingly unafraid of what had been going on outside.

Nikki said, "You look a little rough."

Stiletto cleared his throat. "Is this what you've been doing the whole time?"

"No. I started in the conference room with the other monkeys, and when the shooting started, I decided to see what I could find in here that might help you guys. You know, the secret files as stuff that are always laying around, and there was Mrs. Minas ready to go, but really upset that her husband hadn't come for her first."

"Where is the fat bastard?" Mrs. Minas asked.

"Out on the grass. Dead."

"Did you kill him?"

"I helped," Stiletto said.

"Serves him right." Clarissa Minas saluted the air with her glass and downed what remained. Swallowing, she let out a burp. Then she started to laugh.

"Tell you what," the woman said after she'd stopped laughing. "Let me finish this bottle, then I'll show you where all the files and stuff are. Oh, and you need to find General Florez."

"Who?"

"The man in charge of the army," Mrs. Minas said. "He wanted to kill Lazaro and take over. My husband never figured it out, but I knew. I could tell. Anyway, if he's still alive, he might be a problem later."

"We'll go look."

"Can't miss him. Got a big fruit thing on his chest. He's proud of his medals." She laughed again.

Stiletto turned and left the two women to their girl talk or whatever they wanted to call it. He hadn't counted on Mrs. Minas being anything but in the way of a bullet when it was all said and done, but Nikki Fortune keeping her entertained might prove useful if the woman knew where Minas kept his records and other information that might help stabilize Venezuela in the coming days. And weeks. And months.

The shooting might be over, but the war was far from finished. There was plenty of work for Verduzco and his soldiers to accomplish.

Smoke still hung in the air outside, and there was a lot of shouting from the front of the building. Stiletto headed that way.

Two rebel soldiers stood near the fountain in the center courtyard of the palace, with a dead man propped between them. The dead man wore a general's uniform with "a big fruit thing" on his chest—his collection of medals.

Carlos Verduzco snapped a picture. Then he had to take another one because the general's bloody head slipped from the hand of one of the rebels propping him up. Once the head was straight, they took the second picture. The dead man's face was half-gone.

Stiletto found Colonel Verduzco nearby, observing.

"Is that General Florez?" Stiletto asked.

"The late general, yes. The man responsible for more death and destruction than Minas."

Stiletto thought back to the farm he and Beth had arrived at as soon as their cargo plane had crashed. The dead family with the flies buzzing around them. Had the general ordered their murders? Probably. Stiletto decided a sense of justice had finally descended on the troubled land. Wounds might never heal, but at least the former victims had a chance to take back control.

There were other bodies scattered around the courtyard, too. Stiletto couldn't help but notice one of the dead men, laying there like discarded trash, had stitches on his head. The killer from Miami. The man who had killed Stiletto's driver the night of the party. Scott may have been denied the opportunity to punch the man's ticket, but he'd met his end the same way as he'd lived. That was enough.

"Hear from Arencibia?"

"All's well. They took the television station, and have been broadcasting my message about the coup. We are in control now."

"Congratulations, Mr. President."

Verduzco snapped his eyes to Stiletto. "I am not—" He stopped and sighed. "How did you know?"

"I never believed for a minute that you had somebody waiting in the wings. It was always you."

"Or my son."

"That, too."

"But neither of us have been elected. I'm not assuming power."

"No, but you'll get the big chair."

"And the first thing I will do," Verduzco said, looking around at the V-shaped monstrosity, "is knock down this eyesore. It looks like a Motel 6."

"That joke was barely funny the first time, Colonel."

Verduzco took a deep breath. "Thank you for bringing my son back to me. I might have neglected to say so before."

"You didn't, but you're welcome."

"You could have left us. Your mission was done. We had the medicine, and you had the CIA agents. Why did you stay?"

"Because it was the right thing to do."

"If you ever need refuge, a place to stay, anything—"

"Caracas will be my first stop," Stiletto said. He extended his hand. Colonel Verduzco clasped it tightly.

"Very good, my friend," the rebel leader said.

As night descended on Venezuela, celebrations broke out around the country, the citizens enjoying their first taste of true freedom in a very long time.

Rebel units remained active to put down resistance from surviving army forces, but the call for surrender had mostly been answered positively. The major portion of the army that sided with the rebels helped bring their comrades to task.

Members of the various branches of government and political parties had either pledged their support to the change in government or gone into hiding. There were so many corrupt politicians in the government, they had nowhere to hide now that their protection had been removed. Those not corrupt brought up the incoming United Nations inspectors and proposed that a new visit to New York City was in order to update the Security Council on the latest. They would plead not only for the money promised, but for more help in getting Venezuela back on her feet.

The gangsters who had been planning nefarious activities with the late Lazaro Minas were confined to their hotel rooms. They would be deported as soon as the rebels re-opened the airport.

Stiletto, vouching for Nikki Fortune, had managed to keep her from the forced confinement, although she had nowhere else to go but her hotel while the main business was sorted. Stiletto promised to look in on her later.

Beth Carrington checked in with The Trust in Zurich to make a report. Melissa Jarrett explained their efforts to trace the leak that resulted in the shoot-down of the DC-10.

After explaining the background details, she told Beth that information found in Ramon Salazar's home had pointed to direct communication with Lazaro Minas, as well as a minor player at the CIA's Central American desk, who would soon be visited by agents of the FBI to answer to charges of espionage. Jarrett added that Jenny Farnsworth, whom Beth had met once or twice before, would be let go from The Trust. She was innocent as far as the security breach was concerned, but her carelessness had almost cost agents their lives. Number One could not tolerate that. Beth passed the information on to Stiletto, who took the news in stride. With everything else going on, he hadn't given much thought to what The Trust was up to.

The next morning, Sergeant Castillo drove Stiletto in a Jeep back to the church where they had left Tim Pierce, the CIA man, and two other former island prisoners who had been too injured to continue the journey after the escape.

Father Dominick waited for them in front of the building. He stood in the shade of a large tree near the building.

Stiletto hopped out of the Jeep and shook the priest's hand.

"We won, padre," Stiletto said.

"Good," Father Dom replied. "Maybe Venezuela will know peace once again. It is a beautiful country."

"Which is why it was a shame to scar it the way we have, but there was no other choice."

"You don't need to justify your efforts to me."

Stiletto laughed self-consciously. If not the priest, who was he trying to convince?

He let the question pass.

"I guess it's an old habit."

Father Dom looked sad.

"Are we too late?" Stiletto asked. He knew the look.

"I'm afraid your American friend left us last night."

Stiletto's shoulders fell.

"We have the body wrapped, and he will be ready to transport back to the United States when you leave."

Stiletto sighed.

"He asked a favor of you, didn't he?"

Stiletto cleared his throat. "He did. I have to go tell his daughter what happened. But I don't know what to tell her."

"He told me you had a daughter too?"

"I do."

"What would you tell your own daughter?"

"A lot of things. So many things."

If she'd only talk to me. For five minutes. . .

"I think you'll figure out what you need to say, and when."

Stiletto felt weak, as if the weight he carried had suddenly increased and his legs would buckle under the strain. He started to breathe faster. Father Dom put a strong hand on his right shoulder.

"You do what you do for a reason," the father said. "People depend on you. They have nobody else."

Stiletto almost choked out the words, "It's harder than I thought."

For the first time since his wife died, he felt like crying.

"You were chosen," the priest said. "And you're strong enough. When your time is over and another takes your place, everything unsettled will be put right."

Stiletto managed a laugh. His vision was blurred. "You heard that directly?"

Father Dom smiled but didn't answer the question. He said, "Right now, you're tired. You'll have a different perspective after you've had some rest. And some time. Don't rush to the next battle."

Stiletto nodded. He sniffed.

Father Dom pulled a photograph out of a pocket. Pierce's daughter. Stiletto took the picture.

"I wrote her address on the back."

Stiletto turned the picture over. On the back, neatly written, was all the information Scott needed.

Father Dom called to a trio of young men digging

nearby in a garden and told them to bring the body of the American to the Jeep, and get the other rebel prisoners ready for transport as well. To Stiletto, he said, "Go sit. We'll take it from here."

Stiletto returned to the Jeep in a daze. Castillo handed him a canteen. Stiletto took a long drink and handed it back.

"I'm sorry," the sergeant said.

Stiletto wiped his eyes. "We tried."

Sometimes, that was all you could do.

But he would do more than try with the request the CIA man had made. Tim Pierce, a person Stiletto barely knew, but a man who had thought highly of him, had asked Scott to carry a message, and Stiletto planned to follow through.

No matter the cost.

No matter the strain.

Because someday, he might need somebody to do the same thing for him.

And as the young men carried the body of CIA agent Tim Pierce out of the church on a stretcher, Stiletto knew what his next mission would be.

The hardest mission ever.

IF YOU LIKED THIS BOOK, CHECK OUT RETRIBUTION BY BRENT TOWNS

EVERYTHING COMES AT A COST...

Author Brent Towns keeps the action coming thick and fast, let's you up for a breath and then drags you back in for more.

After he is betrayed and shoots the two most powerful men in the Irish Mob, John "Reaper" Kane is forced into hiding. He thinks Retribution, Arizona, is the perfect hiding place, but he is wrong. Underneath the old, crusty surface of the dying town, hides the Montoya Cartel, for they use it as a funnel to ship their drugs across the border.

Trying to lay low in a town gripped with lawlessness is impossible for the ex-recon marine, especially after the local sheriff is brutally murdered by the Montoya Cartel's sicario, leaving an old friend, Deputy Sheriff Cara Billings, the only person standing between them and the town.

Things go from bad to worse when Kane is arrested by Cleaver, the deputy in the cartel's pocket, for shooting a local gang member.

Enter DEA Agent Luis Ferrero who has expressed to his bosses for a long time the need for a task force to fight the cartels on their own ground. He's about to get his wish, and to head up his team, he wants the Reaper.

A thrill ride that doesn't let you go – Retribution is the first novel in the action-packed Reaper Series.

AVAILABLE NOW ON AMAZON

ABOUT THE AUTHOR

A twenty-five year veteran of radio and television broad-casting, Brian Drake has spent his career in San Francisco where he's filled writing, producing, and reporting duties with stations such as KPIX-TV, KCBS, KQED, among many others. Currently carrying out sports and traffic reporting duties for Bloomberg 960, Brian Drake spends time between reports and carefully guarded morning and evening hours cranking out action/adventure tales.

Brian Drake lives in California with his wife and two cats, and when he's not writing he is usually blasting along the back roads in his Corvette with his wife telling him not to drive so fast, but the engine is so loud he usu-ally can't hear her.

You will find him regularly blogging at:
www.briandrake88.blogspot.com